To Raise Another World:
A Sequel

The Eight and Another
in the
Archerland Series

H. R. Coursen

Just Write Books

© 2008 H. R. Coursen

Library of Congress Catalog Card No.: 2007924341

Coursen, H. R.
To Raise Another World; a novel/H. R. Coursen
p. 124
1. Fantasy-General—Fiction. 2. Religion—Fiction.
1. Title.

ISBN: 978-0-9788628-4-8

Published by

𝕵𝖂𝕭

Just Write Books
Topsham, Maine 04086
207-729-3600 • jstwrite@jstwrite.com
Printed in the United States of America

Other Books by H. R. Coursen

Archerland: The Series

For Susan, Bruce, Maggie and Katey

God vouchsafes to raise another world (*Paradise Lost* XI 876).

Whichever way I fly is hell; myself am hell (*Paradise Lost* IV 75).

God chooses not to captivate under a perpetual childhood, but ... trusts him with the gift of reason to be his own chooser. (*Areopagitica*).

Indeed one man cannot do all things, nor even hope to do all. (*Lament for Damon*).

Or, if Virtue feeble were, Heaven itself would stoop to her. (*Comus*).

Dramatis Personae

Estrella, formerly a General in the Army of Archerland and once Commander of the Royal Stone Brigade.

Her sons, Harry and George, also the sons of the late George Mazlund, who was killed in battle against his father, Mazlund, Prince of the Underworld and one of the chief fallen angels.

Mazlund.

Jerome the Gnome.

Lisle, formerly of Mazlund's palace staff. Jerome's friend.

Tomaso, formerly Troll of the Bridge, still a Troll.

Cybella, formerly a wood-spirit living in a tree by a pool. Grunius freed her.

Grunius, a star-reader and a reader of horizons. Friend of Cybella.

Umgalla, Chief of the Native Inhabitants of Otherland.

Majorum, Daughter of Umgalla.

Blackie, a cat.

Sheba, a large dog, descendant of Major, the great white dog who accompanied young Paul (later King Paul I) on his adventures long ago.

Neutralon, Prince of Enclava.

Seraman, an opportunist who undergoes frequent changes of heart, occasionally for the better.

Langar, brother of the late King Mark of Archerland, an opportunistic accomplice of Mazlund's.

Glorimere, former Queen of Archerland, in exile in her native Leetops as this narrative begins.

Gregg, a fisherman, friend of Glorimere.

Chirac, Mazlund's wine steward and butler.

Hector, once a great warrior of Troy.

Mazlund's Lieutenants: von Beak, von Rodent, Vallarte, and Heinz.

Native Warriors, Guards of the Fortress, Soldiers, Members of Mazlund's Blackfeather Patrol and a Flyer of Umgalla's Raptor Squadron.

I.

The waters where the battle had taken place had turned red at the point where the River of the Green Eyes met the sea. The setting sun had seemed to stretch further for an instant to become this place where so many had died. Then a green radiance had flashed from the sky and given a final light to the armor of the fallen soldiers, heads down in the rising tide. And the waters had risen over the fallen spears, the broken swords, the torn reins, the blackened mouths of the cannon, the shattered helmets, the rounded flanks of the dead horses, the red of the blood of horse and man. That had been the last tide to wash across those shores. The land itself had trembled like the back of an angry animal and been swallowed in a great foaming mouth without a head. All signs of the battle had sunk, as had the hovels and cottages, the gleaming parapets and proud palaces of Archerland. Now, some of the high turrets stood many fathoms beneath the smooth surface of the sea, long weeds riding like pennons in the shrug of an ocean at a depth to which the light barely reached. Fishes with huge eyes swam through windows that once had looked down upon courtyards far below, windows now sightless above the murk of the bottom of the sea.

Archerland, which had fallen from God, was no more.

Mazlund, who had also fallen from God at the precise moment when history was beginning, signaled his formation. Left bank. Roll. Dive. The squadron timed its roll-over – one-thousand one, one-thousand two — and followed Mazlund downward toward the sea. Mazlund had to be careful, of course. With only one eye, his depth-perception was not good and he had to check the horizon again and again to time his pull-out from the split-s of his dive. He did not want his entire formation to follow him into the water at a speed that would be fatal to even the hardiest of crows.

Yes! Twigs and leaves still green, no doubt from some rain storm that had driven them into a river and from thence into the sea. They were close to land! And, not a moment too soon! His squadron was tired and hungry. Now, if they could avoid the patrolling gulls likely to be guarding the shore, they could land, rest, feed, and make plans.

Plans? What plans? Ever since his first plan, none had gone right. Well, this time things would be different.

> "No, Mazlund, Never!
> It is ever your desire
> to leap from the fire
> that burns inside your soul.
> But you know that your role
> is forever to try.
> Forever! You cannot die!"

He shook for a moment along his hollow bones. This crow-being should be oblivious to such thoughts, he thought. But it was not. The pain was more vivid when he assumed his human shape, of course. As a crow, he suffered merely a dull ache accompanied by short, rhyming couplets that coincided with the up and down beat of his wings.

The two rafts, tied together with a few circles of rope secured by a bowline, had seemed solid enough on the calm ocean. Now, as the swells rose in their back and forth commerce with the shore, the rafts bent apart and then crunched together, throwing their occupants almost into the water and then tipping them into each other.

"We won't make it!" Lisel cried.

"What can we do?" Jerome the Gnome asked, of no one in particular.

They were about to enter the surf that crashed toward the bright line of beach in front of the trees. But that beach, so close, also seemed impossibly distant, and more dangerous the closer they got.

"All of us!" Jerome cried, answering his question, "Off the raft! Hold on to the back end, away from the shore!"

No one moved.

"Yes!" said the Troll of the Bridge, whose name was Tomaso Del Puente, as the raftmates had learned.

He scuttled toward the back edge of the raft.

"And everyone kick!" Estrella shouted, following Tomaso.

And quickly, all of them, Jerome, Tomaso, Estrella, her sons, George and Henry, and Lisle were holding on for dear life to the cracks in the boards with their fingertips and kicking their feet as the raft, with Sheba and Blackie aboard, rose up and dropped down into the trough.

Sheba gave a sharp bark. Estrella looked over her shoulder.

Yes! The cruising fins, gray and gleaming under the height of the sun, were those of sharks. And — the sharks were close!

It had begun with a feeling for which no word existed. Once he had lived in his human shape for a while, Mazlund had recognized it as boredom. He was to experience long stretches – thousands of years – of boredom punctuated by moments of exhilaration when he thought he had a battle won and instants of sheer rage when he recognized one more time that he had lost. Yes, the constant adoration of the illumination known those days (although no days existed, or nights) as Jehovah was simply dull. Of course, Mazlund could not say that word, the "J" word. Even the thought was hurtful to him, a twist in the gut. That experience known as pain needs contrast, Mazlund knew, but the constant worship of the central light had been pre-experiential, as he also knew. But as he looked at his fellow seraphs circling in a great, luminous row around the shining one, he could tell that they were bored (although the word did not yet exist and the concept itself was just coming into being). Their great folded wings yearned for employment. Their eyes wished to close occasionally, or at least to look at the shadows that played along the bottom of a stream or watch the way leaves turned white-side-up when the winds changed direction. But no streams or trees existed, nor any wind except that whirled out by a few Cherubim who stooged around, waiting to be given a message to deliver. But no one sent any messages. What was there to say?

One day, Mazlund caught a glint of light from the seraph next to him, Lucifer. Was it just the heatless oxidation that made Lucifer glow? No. Something else.

"You too?" Mazlund muttered.

The archangel nodded slightly, and the cosmos – as yet undifferentiated matter — shook. Had anyone been able to observe it, he or she would have seen a slant of light flash toward the two, Mazlund, then named Illumio, and Lucifer. The light rushed back to its source then downward in the darkness below. Jehovah thought the concept of space and made in it a place where light carried heat with it, a place of fire.

Suddenly, Lucifer and Illumio and a host of others near them discovered that Jehovah had thought of something much later to be named gravity. They were falling down through a space-time continuum, going almost (but not quite) at the speed of light – though they tried for it in their panicky wish to get back to where they had been. Their great wings were on fire, burning down the many years of darkness in a tumble seemingly without end that sent sparks and random skeletons of feathers in brief red fragments upward in a trail that went out of sight as the fallen ones kept falling.

They crashed at last in great spatterings of blue embers but did not achieve the escape of death. Mazlund, recognizing his new name without being told, realized that he had left his old name somewhere above him. Well, he'd recall it once he recovered from this long descent.

"It's all about naming," he said, rising and batting some random hotspots from one of his wings with the other. He looked up at the endless trail of blue smoke above him.

"No," said Lucifer. "It is about essence."

And Mazlund felt the change in him.

"At least I am no longer bored," he said.

"A magnificent rationalization," Lucifer replied.

And Mazlund realized that he could not remember the name he had borne before his fall. And he found that he could not say the name of the power on which he had gazed for so long. He felt pain when he became aware that that name and what it represented still existed.

"So," said Lucifer, "what will come to be known as history has begun."

"And so?"

"And so, you fool, we make mischief where once the status quo was king."

"That's not all," Mazlund said.

"I know that! Do you think that I who looked upon the source of all that is do not know what I have lost?"

Mazlund discovered that he did not like being called a fool. He felt the radiation echoing out from the explosion that the unnamed whatever had caused. And so he had come to Archerland, a small island kingdom that would offer no resistance to his sovereignty. That had been two thousand years ago, an eyeblink as eternity is measured, or not measured. He knew that while time and space are finite, their edges cannot be found. They exist at the vanishing point where they intersect with the mind of the force that he could not name.

Neutralon stepped into a small boat at the harborside of Enclava. He untied the painter and floated free just as the water flowed over the wharf from which he had stepped. Soon he was looking down at the gray boards of the fishing village below him. Shingles pulled loose and spun upward. Glass shattered like ice in a springtime river, and pilings that had stood above the tide for hundreds of years came loose, rising to the surface and leaping upward, like angry crocodiles, in a lash of white water before they settled sullenly along this spreading sea. The gray backs of fish flickered in the muddy dust below.

Neutralon regretted leaving his tapestry behind him. It had been capable of weaving the future into its threads and had permitted him to avoid many unpleasant moments, located as he was in a zone frequently occupied by Mazlund's Darkcorps. The tapestry had even predicted his own hanging – or, at least, had shown him emerging from a prison toward a gallows in the town square – but that hempen moment had been interrupted by a timely intervention. He touched his throat, then looked around the small boat. Yes, a mast and sail. He would pull them up and see where the wind took him. Sooner or later he would find a shore. And meanwhile he assumed that he would acquire a taste for raw meat.

II.

Mazlund banked toward an old-growth stand of oak.

"Crowl!" he called, and his squadron swung from echelon to in-trail behind him.

They twisted down, a thin, black ribbon that interrupted the light, and landed in a field beside the woods, claws out, wings tilted at a radical dihedral to brake their movement.

"Squalk! Crowl! Squalk!"

"D'Nulzam!"

Mazlund stood in his former glory, hussar's short jacket, blue velvet and braided in gold, Order of the Spider, First Class held by a ribbon below his throat.

Von Beak and von Rodent stood beside him, each wearing the Order of the Rat, First Class, and the Iron Crow, First Class, inferior decorations at which Mazlund sneered. He was the only one to hold the Order of the Spider.

"We await your orders, Master of Malignity," von Beak said.

What orders? Mazlund wondered.

"We will find out what is here," he said. "What people. If any. Who governs them. What grapes may be available for fermentation. Then we will plan to subvert the government and win the people to our cause."

"Let us hope that they are not like those of Archerland," von Rodent said.

Mazlund's ever-angry eye shot him an even angrier glance from the pin-prick of a single pupil.

"You don't enjoy a challenge?"

"I don't enjoy defeat, Prince of Perverse Practices and Sundry Insalubrities."

Von Rodent knew that the way to Mazlund's heart – if that's what it was – was in bestowing honorifics upon him.

"And, Regent of Ruthless Wrath and Resultant Wreckage, I do aspire to that certificate of the Unholy Order of Arachnidia and its attendant device."

Mazlund fingered the medal at his throat.

"We will see."

It was a good idea to encourage ambition in his subordinates, even if he had no intention of conferring the decoration on anyone but himself. Still, if he chose to confer this particular medal, he could design and designate a higher order.

"Send out scouts!" he ordered.

Von Beak saluted, turned, and pointed.

"You, you, and you."

"D'Nulzam," said each of the soldiers.

And, as the others watched, bony beaks emerged from noses, eyes grew black and slid to the side of slender skulls, and feathers slid out from pores, blue-black in the slant of afternoon.

"Squalk! Crowl! Squawl! Scree!" von Beak ordered.

The great crows shrugged from their epaulets and lumbered into the air, leaving empty uniforms and boots rumpled idly along the field.

"They will return in an hour," von Beak said.

"I heard the order," Mazlund snarled.

"Kick harder!" Estrella shouted, just as she swallowed a mouthful of salt.

The flotilla of sharks circled away from this augmented splashing, but then turned back with a simultaneous, sinuous thrust.

At that moment, the combined boards with their human occupants clinging to them and kicking with all their might with legs of varying lengths, rose upward within the gray wall of a swell, then teetered for an instant in space.

"Hang on!" Jerome shouted, as much to himself as to his companions. He was about to be pulled forward under one of the rafts. He pushed his arms against it, feeling his legs tugged in the other direction.

The sharks were in target-selection mode.

Tomaso the Troll felt his short fingers slip from the boards of the raft. Without a word, he disappeared.

And then the wave crashed and the boards rushed toward the shore. The sharks circled away, shadows under the green after-wash of the wave.

The human survivors crawled up the strand, sand and stones pressing past their hands and kneecaps as water moved back toward its destiny as wave again. Sheba pranced onto the beach without getting her paws wet, while Blackie remained on the boards, now high and dry, watching the others with her neutral yellow eyes and licking a paw.

Estrella stood, coughing the bitter taste of salt from her lungs and did a quick count with her eyes.

The great wave had picked Tomaso up and flung him ashore ahead of the raft.

"All here!"

"So it seems," said Lisle, giving Jerome a hand so that he could find his feet again.

"I lost my hat," said Tomaso, Troll of the Bridge.

"Yes," said Estrella, "we will need some protection against this sun. It seems warmer than the one that shone in Archerland."

"Do we know where we are?" Cybella asked.

"South and east of where we were," Grunius said. "I'll know more when I can look at the stars."

Cybella paused to watch some birds flying along the surf.

"Ruddy Turnstones, flying north to nest."

"Let us go inland and find some fresh water," Estella said.

"That's easy!" said George. "See that space between the trees? It's a stream."

"Yes," said Harry, not to be outdone. "There's a gap there along the shore where it runs down to the sea!"

And soon they were seated by a shaded pool a short way from the shore but out of sight and sound of the restless waves.

"I wonder whether this pool has a resident deity," Cybella asked.

"Perhaps," Grunius said. "I feel a presence. But she would be very unlikely to reveal herself amid a host of strangers."

"How well I know!" Cybella said.

"Bless her, wherever she is!" Lisle said.

They drank of the cool waters and washed the crust of salt from their hands and faces. It was a pause in which each of them had a chance to ponder their delivery from the wild waters and its predators. But – what now?

Estrella realized that they were looking to her. Of course – I am the highest ranking person here, a commander in the citizen-army of Archerland. But that was there in the land now sunk beneath the sea, drowned with its hierarchies, the rankings of things and of people, structures deemed necessary to cope with what happens everyday, and believed essential in the fight against Mazlund. But this is another dispensation altogether!

And until they worked out a better system, she thought, I had better continue to make decisions. And, at least, we do not have Mazlund with whom to contend. Just this wild place and what dangers it may hold within it. That will suffice!

"I say we follow the stream, to higher ground. That way we will be safe from any storms that spring up along these waters. We will set up an encampment near this wonderful fresh water, provided for us by the deities of pool and stream..."

She smiled at Grunius and Cybella.

"...and hunt for small game. We'll have to set up a watch in case of lions..."

"Or bears," Harry said.

"Yes, and..." George paused.

"Other people?" Harry asked.

"We will have to look for them, yes," Estrella said.

"Will they be friendly?" George asked.

"We will offer them no violence," Estrella said. "Let us hope that we do not threaten them."

Mazlund recognized that he still had at his command a small but effective military unit. In his Blackfeather Patrol he had ample surveillance capability, as the text books at Low Point Academy called it, and he had never underestimated the value of an eyes-in-the-sky program. Archerland's Loyal Crow Patrol had often proved to him how dangerous it could be to have the movement and disposition of one's forces relayed to an inevitably smaller army. He had not always understood how an outnumbered adversary could muster its forces where needed, anticipating a flanking action by Mazlund's Midnight Mauraders, his elite cavalry unit, or massing to repel a charge by the Fearsome Phalanx, his usually irresistible infantry, as if the enemy had known precisely where the attack would come. But so it had been.

Now, he thought, I have military superiority over any conceivable enemy! A little heavy on generals and staff officers, he recognized, but at least they would behave from the expertise of failure and from the fear that he could instill even in his most senior commanders, who could scarcely control their hands when Mazlund frowned. The rest of his formations were made up of mercenaries, who enjoyed the elegant uniforms and the ample rations of wine, and were seldom deterred by defeat. They were, after all, well paid. I may have to put in a performance incentive, though, Mazlund thought sourly. They have grown accustomed to this long losing streak.

A crow landed at his feet.

"Speak!"

The crow did not go through the process of reestablishing his human shape.

"Squawl, Squak, Crowl, Squeek, Squalk!"

The thirteen words the crows had could be rearranged in many ways. Crowspeak, like the other language of Mazlund's Spystaffle – the scouting branch of his Blackfeather Patrol — Seagullese, was a word-order language.

"Really?" Mazlund said, more in exclamation than in question. "Others have been here before us. Good news!"

The crow reassumed his human identity, shoulders spreading, claws filling out to toes, legs thickening, face rising and taking on flesh as eyes slid to the center, one each beside the nose that shaped over the bony beak, feathers stinging back into the pores from which they had been extruded only a half-hour before.

"The fortress has been abandoned for a long time, Nabob of Nasty Surprises, but its keep is intact and its dungeons ample."

"Good! Good! A successful state cannot function without ample dungeons!"

Mazlund glanced at von Rodent, who clenched his fists.

Mazlund laughed within himself. Even my mildest look is a threat!

"And, Master of Malignity, its wine cellar is intact, though deep in dust!"

"Even better!" Mazlund said, running his tongue over his upper lip. "Although I doubt that these vintages will excel the Soauve of Lucidia, which had the temerity to smile with its aftertaste at its own dry wit. Eh – von Beak?"

"Why... ah no... Caliph of Calamity."

Mazlund enjoyed twitting his two Generals. He himself was the only officer who held the rank of Field Marshall.

"Perhaps it has all turned to vinegar," muttered von Rodent sourly.

"What optimism!" Mazlund said.

"I have long since surrendered my romantic view of the world," von Rodent replied.

"And with good reason!" Mazlund said, laughing. "My followers, let us proceed to the fortress that Heinz here has discovered. For you, Heinz, the Blue Crow – and with oatmeal cluster — if the wine turns out to be potable!"

Captain Heinz held his right arm out to Mazlund.

"I am grateful, Lord of Lightning."

"And Thunder!" Mazlund corrected, the rebuke in his voice retrained only by his sudden need for a good wine. He had built up a thirst!

"Come! Captain Heinz, lead the way!"

Langar shouted in panic as the tiny cockleshell was pulled into the backwash of a wave.

Not so brave now! Seraman thought. He does well in the field with a battle-stallion under him and a broadsword in his hand, but not here at sea. Well, he thought, different people have different fears. He had better not tell Langar about the dorsal fins he had spotted slicing the waters just outside the uproll of the breakers.

Seraman had no time to congratulate himself on his own calmness. The tiny raft was engulfed in the crushing pressure of a crashing wave and the roar in his ears and the scrape of liquid sand against his closed eyes blotted out all thoughts except one – is this the moment when the world I have created through my eyes and ears and that I continue to create for a moment or two more turns into darkness and silence? He waited to find out.

"Oh!" cried Langar as the tiny craft tipped upwards and slid down the inner half of a breaking wave.

"Hold on!" Seraman shouted. But that was to himself. He should have told Langar to let go. The raft rushed inward, bouncing against the chop returning from the shore. And he was still aboard. Breathing. And, yes, so was Langar. Also breathing. Well, Seraman thought, there's a downside to not drowning in the surf near this unknown land.

"We establish here!" Mazlund said. "Von Beak, do you still have your black battle flag with the albino crow in its center?"

"I do, Majordomo of Malevolence."

"Bring it! It will fly from these parapets."

As the flag took to the wind, Mazlund looked at his small circle.

"In the name of all that is unholy, in honor of all that thrives under rocks, in the name of all unhallowed zones where lurk the instruments of evil and where are imprisoned all lost souls, we raise our eyes to this dark flag. We will not yield until it flies over all the world!"

"Nema," muttered his followers.

"No. They seem more in need of help themselves than posing any threat to us."

"Could they be deceiving us, Markum?"

"I doubt it, Umgalla. For one thing, they don't even know we are here."

"Yes. That is true."

"And, for another, they don't know where they are. They seem not to have come here voluntarily. They've been washed up from the sea after escaping from some sinking ship."

"A ship?"

"They have that ship-wrecked look about them."

"Thank you, Markum."

The young man held his right fist up to Umgalla and left the building, a long house constructed of bent branches covered with bearhide.

Umgalla sat in thought. His ancestors had told of men with light skin and suits of shining metal landing on these shores. They had made slaves of the native inhabitants, forcing them to quarry the rock for the Fortress that had been built two valleys away. Some natives had been servants in that place, bringing food to the light-skinned strangers. Other natives had been forced to give these men the crops that they grew and the game that they hunted. The men in metal suits said they had come for gold. They became very angry when Umgalla's ancestors would not tell them where gold was to be found. After all, Umgalla's forebears did not know what gold was. At last, these strangers returned to the great ship that had brought them – they called it a galleon – and had sailed away without their gold, leaving the starving natives behind. The tribe had almost become extinct, but had survived and grown hardy with the generations.

And then another group had come – only a sunrise or two ago – and had occupied the Fortress. Umgalla was suspicious of them. They had the eyes of rats, he thought, dark and darting, and they seemed to prefer the night, when most of nature slept, to the light of day. That, too, was like the rat. As yet, this group had not threatened Umgalla and his small tribe. But that was, he thought, because he and his followers had avoided these ominous people – if people they were – who seemed content to rebuild and refurbish the Fortress before they made incursions on the land around it.

And now, this further group. Survivors rather than invaders, Markum had surmised.

Well, Umgalla would have a look for himself.

"Let us pause for a moment," Estrella said.

The others gathered around her.

"We have come to a new land. Our own is lost. Whatever powers may be looking over us – those of the Living Lord, whom we hope is ever-present, and perhaps those indigenous to this place, we ask your guidance. Winter will come. Help us prepare for it. We are of this new land. Help us to celebrate its presence in our lives and our uninvited presence in its life. This we ask in the name of whatever larger spirit animates this land and its creatures."

"Amen!" called the others.

They then resumed their work on their camp on a level space beside the stream. They built a fire against the cooling twilight.

"Just fallen wood and twigs," Cybella said. "Nothing alive."

"We will have to hunt," Grunius said.

"Of course," Cybella said. "One of the necessities that the natural world forces upon us."

"Our supplies will last us for a few more days," said Jerome.

"A miracle!" Estrella said.

"The result of the process of wave action on something that floats," said Grunius.

"We can make bows and arrows," George said.

"And set traps," Harry said.

"I will make myself a new hat," said Tomaso.

"You will be our leader," Lisle said to Estrella.

The others nodded.

"I have thought of that," Estrella said. "Yes, I will make some decisions. But we are no longer in Archerland. We belong to this new land now. We have been delivered, I would assert, by the living God, but, as Jerome reminded me on the raft – that seems a long time ago! – some of our compatriots were not delivered. I am willing to accept a world in which spirits still abide in trees, as they did in remote parts of Archerland, and in streams, and in groves that rise like the columns of a temple. So we will not debate comparative theology when we have such pressing things to do. We can believe what we choose to believe if that faith sustains us now. I will make decisions, but I will submit them to you, our community, for your response. We must decide for the good of each of us and all of us and for the good of those who choose to join us. Any disagreements will be resolved by your voices. And each of you has one voice. That includes me. We may decide that we need some military – for defense, of course – in which case we would nominate leaders. And those leaders would have authority in the event of an emergency. We might not have time to debate such an emergency. We might have to respond instantly to orders, as we have done in the past. Is it agreed that we form a community, here established under the aegis of the Living Lord, whom we know is strong, and of whatever other system of higher power may exist in this unknown place, and that each of us has a single voice in the making of future decisions?"

The group nodded.

"Let me hear your voices," Estrella said.

"Aye," came the voices.

"Any dissent?"

A distant rumble of thunder was the only reply.

"Always someone!" Estrella said, laughing. "But since clouds are on the move, I suggest that we make ourselves shelters from the fallen branches of these giant pine trees, and that we set a guard, and then the rest of us sleep after this trying day, but one that has given us a beginning here."

But the tucket of thunder gave her pause. Could she be sure that the Living Lord, having forsaken them in Archerland, had followed them with benevolent intention to this unknown place? And, of course, she corrected, it was we who did the forsaking!

"Can I be a guard?" Harry asked.

"May I?" Estrella corrected. "Of course. Volunteers are always welcome."

"And I," said Tomaso.

"What?" Estrella asked.

"Whatever needs doing," Tomaso said.

But, having volunteered, he wondered what it was that he, a weak-eyed Troll who had spent his life under a bridge could possibly do to help this group of refugees. Jerome the Gnome wondered also. Long ago he had guarded the Mines, and he had been a great spy in his time, but what use had this group for his skills in espionage? And where were any mines to guard?

And soon the others were on the edge of sleep, their eyes rocked gently by the imagery of their recent adventure in the sea.

III

"The horizon is not easy to read," Grunius said.

"Why?" asked Cybella.

"In Archerland, the horizon had a sea behind it."

"What difference does that make?"

"Perspective. Contrast. We see white flowers against a background of green. When we dream, we often dream of being under water."

"Yes. I do have such dreams."

"And what do you find there?"

"You are answering me with a question."

"Of course."

"I find there the great beams of ships being eaten by worms that feast on wood, and in the dim light, I see pearls scattered from shattered trunks, pale and gleaming like the glint of dead fish trapped in rocks at the bottom of a lake. And, lately, I see the stones of our kingdom, some strewn at random, others still holding together in towers that once seemed to climb above the clouds. I see hope and loss of hope."

"Yes," said Grunius. "You see the future interrupted: a ship that never reached its port, the past empty of its former meanings, and buildings empty of their people. You were the spirit of the oak tree for such a long time. But when I look at a horizon backed by the sea I sense the past rising and reflecting what the future holds. I must differentiate between the two times that summon themselves to the edge of the world. Here, though, the horizon gleams between the trees, and it is a different text. But, then, the stars..."

"Yes. They tell another story."

"They tell the same story, but in a different way."

"Why does this horizon...?"

"It will speak to me. But I have to learn its language. I do see smoke there, in the distance."

"Fire?"

"Not wild-fire, no. The smoke that cooks food and warms homes."

"We are not alone?"

"No."

"Is that a fear?"

"I am not yet sure."

"Will the stars tell you?"

"Perhaps. It depends upon what they say. The stars are like our dreams, except that when we look at them we have our eyes open to the universe that extends so vastly out from where we stand."

"And with our eyes closed we look at the universe that extends so vastly within us."

"True, and we must observe and then interpret."

"I think this new world is good for us," Cybella said. "We had come to take the other place for granted. I had, at least."

"Yes," Grunius replied. "We believe that nothing happens unless we are there. It is almost as if we give events our permission. But that is our own arrogance. Because it was not observed does not mean that an event did not occur. We come across a fallen tree. Did an ear vibrate when it fell? Did the lens of an eye record its downward crashing as roots surrendered to the greater weight above and ripped the earth into a wound? The event was independent of human senses and quite apart from any action of any god. It happened. It was nature that includes us but is quite a bit larger and exists quite well without us. In fact, probably better, since we tend to take from it."

"We give back!"

"We do. Does Mazlund?"

"No. He is rapacious, a mere predator who does nothing to balance the give and take of the natural world. But even without our presence, the roots would reach for water, the leaves would come out like infant fists opening. And they would lose their grip in autumn."

"And the snow would come."

"Yes, and only the wind would be able to move," said Cybella. "One of the elements of our current existence that I will particularly enjoy will be its slow pace. We see the sun rise and the sun set. It measures our days. The stars inform us of the day to come. The seasons define our activities..."

"Yes, to huddle by a fire."

"There can be a time for that," she said, smiling.

"If one has someone to huddle with."

"Yes. Or to plant seed. And watch it find its way out of the springtime earth. Archerland had become too fast-paced, as if it recognized in its roots and rocks how little time it had left."

"You don't think we are rationalizing?" Grunius asked.

"No. To say that a setback is an opportunity can be a rationalization. This space quivers with possibility."

"A second chance."

"Or a third, or a fourth. If we are careful."

"Yes," said Grunius. "I feel it!

> The Queen Anne's Lace nods at me.
> The blossoms feed the honey bee.
> The golden-rod is a weather vane.
> The wind is from the south again."

Soon, Umgalla, with two of his followers, was observing the camp for himself from the silent shadows of a grove of spruce.

Yes, Marcum had been right. These people were trying to survive. And they were people. Their eyes did not have that suspicious snap of the rat-eyed men in the Fortress.

Motioning his companions forward with a confident smile, Umgalla approached the guard standing on the path where it entered the encampment. This was a crucial moment, he knew, but one that had to be confronted. One of the most dangerous times that existed, as sequence is measured, was when one approached a sentry.

"Who goes?"

Umgalla recognized the language. It had come down to him from his ancestors, who had learned it when they had been slaves generations before.

"A friend."

"Approach."

"Three friends," Umgalla corrected.

Estrella rose and looked toward the edge of the encampment, where her son, Harry, and the three natives stood. She looked at the oldest of them, gray lines of age, like cobwebs, crossing his sun-bronzed face.

She held her right hand up.

"The rest of you, stay here," she commanded.

"But..."

"No voices will be heard on this," she said. "Stay!"

She walked across the clearing, still holding her hand up.

"We are here in peace," she said.

Umgalla held up his right hand, palm forward.

"Peace!"

"And peace be unto you," Estrella said to him. "Come, enter our compound, humble though it be."

"We, too, are a humble people," Umgalla said.

As they took the few paces into the encampment, she looked at the old man who was obviously in charge of the group at his shoulders.

"How do you know our language?"

"It has come down to us from long ago. But that is a long story. Why are you here?"

"We come from another land. We fled as our land sank beneath the waters. We were washed up on your shores. Fortunately."

"You consider it fortunate?"

"Compared to drowning? Compared to starving or dying of thirst? Compared to being burned away by the sun as it fell upon us and glinted back at us from the ocean as we drifted out of sight of shore? Yes, our God brought us here through the workings of His will."

"So you say. My ancestors heard a similar story."

"I would like to hear it."

The survivors of Archerland had retreated to the edge of the encampment at the entrance of the three men, the white-haired old man and his lithe, young companions.

"Yes. I would like to tell you. Tell your people to come forward. We will not harm them."

"I know that," she said.

Estrella waved the small party of Archerland survivors forward to meet these bronze-skinned natives.

"We will feast tomorrow night," said the old man. "And, as the fire dies and falls into its green and gold embers, I will tell you the story."

"That will be interesting to us. We, too have a story."

"And that will interest us."

"And how well you speak our language? I can tell that it is not your native tongue."

"True. Our native tongue incorporates only what you would call nouns and verbs. There are things in this world and there are actions that we take in response to those things."

"Yes. Civilization, as they call it, demands qualification. Nuance."

"We believe that we are a civilized people," Umgalla said.

"I am sure you are. Come sit by the campfire with your two comrades. Were you not civilized, you would have attacked us without warning. Certainly we are vulnerable."

"Yes, but we do not behave that way. Merely because a battle is winnable does not mean that we go to war."

"I admire that philosophy!"

"I will sit with you another time, pale princess. I must now return to my encampment to prepare our people for our feast tomorrow. Come when the warm god of the sky has reached the tops of those trees there."

He pointed toward the west.

"We will be there," Estrella said.

Neutralon gazed over the horizon. His water was running out and he smiled with cracked lips at the irony that sailors often experienced. All this water! But there! Just beyond the green edge that gleamed so enticingly, he saw trees above white sands. Was he hallucinating? No. His eyes had been informed for years by his tapestry. And the wind was blowing him in that direction. What would he find there?

Glorimere's return to Leatops was hardly as festive as had been her sendoff only a year before, when she sailed away to become the Queen of King Mark of Archerland. Mark was dead of a swordthrust from his former friend and lieutenant, Linvallen. They had fought the one and only battle of a civil war on the beach below the River of the Green Eyes. Glorimere had pleaded with Linvallen to flee with her. But no, he, stubborn man, had had his pride, and so had died. Even though she knew that he was gone, her life was an ache for him. Shortly after her boat had embarked from Enclava, Archerland's chief port, the island itself had disappeared. Had anyone else survived? She wondered.

And she asked, was it my fault that I fell in love? Isn't that always the danger in an arranged marriage? Linvallen had been the one dispatched to conduct her to King Mark and the two had fallen in love before they realized what was happening. Well, she thought, that is the nature of love, is it not? She thought so. It had only happened to her that one time.

But whether her fault or not, she was met with a frown by her father, King of Leatops and by a helpless shrug from her mother, the Queen. What – they seemed to ask – are we going to do with you? She was an embarrassment to the royal family and thus to all of Leatops. She often thought that it would have been better had Linvallen not rescued her from the stake on which she was about to be burned and to which she had been walking when he charged in on Crepuscular and snatched her away. To what? To a kind of exile in her own land. She was tolerated, not loved, even by those who had once loved her. She lived far from the bustle and music and high arched ballrooms of the capitol, in a stone cottage overlooking a cliff above the sea that wrinkled like fabric as it worked restlessly against the shore. At the bottom of the hill was a fishing village. She wandered through it alone from time to time, longing for human companionship, but that made things worse. The fishermen were a community in and of themselves, their concerns were the mending of nets, and lines, and the patterns of the fish in various seasons, the chasing of whales away, and the calking of their boats, the ebb and flow of tides. The wives were red-faced and cheerful as they hung their wash and chased their children, but they turned away when Glorimere walked by. Better, she thought, to stay in my cottage staring at the story the fire tells on nights when the chill wind blows in from the sea.

One day, while walking along the quay, she paused to watch a broad-shouldered man rowing toward her. She could not see his face, but she admired the power of his stokes that sent quivering circles away each time he pulled his oars through the smooth green surface. And then the rainbow from the oars as he raised them again above the water! He turned. Instinctively, she took the painter he tossed and secured it to a bollard with a bowline.

It had happened again.

The following evening, as the sun touched the further trees, the small group of Archerland survivors walked to the feast with Umgalla's people across the valley. After the wild turkey, the sweet corn, and the mild, blueberry wine had settled, and as the campfire dwindled toward the golden gashing of fallen logs and was replenished with others, Estrella and Umgalla traded their stories.

Estrella told of Archerland, its kings and queens, its witches and monsters, its towers and olive groves, its combat with the forces of darkness, and how it had fallen away beneath their feet just a short time before.

Umgalla remarked about the young Paul's escape from The Mountains of No Return, "If one can come back when no return can be achieved, then the impossible is possible."

"So we believe," said Estrella, but inwardly she wondered. Do we?

"A battle on the ice?" Umgalla asked. "We know that our rivers freeze at the time that the god-in-the-sky scarcely rises, but we have no zone that is always ice."

"We even had the ice-dwellers help us once."

"And you befriended tigers?"

"One tuft of tigers in the Forests of the Beasts, yes."

"They are not our friends here."

"No," Marcum said, laughing. "They do not become butter at our request!"

"But they keep the woodlands free of scavengers," Umgalla said, "And we do not attack them unless they attack us first. We do, at least, have a truce."

"And your Queen had been a captive in the mines?" Marcum asked.

"Yes. Aprilla, first Queen of the new kingdom that rose from the domination of the Darkforce."

"And young Paul fought a sea-monster in the beast's own grotto with only a hunting knife?"Umgalla asked.

"Yes, and with a wonderful dog called Major."

"It is a powerful story!"

They paused and let the firelight renew itself.

Then, their host began his narrative.

"A long time ago," Umgalla said, still working out the language that he had learned well but had seldom used, "when the ancestors of the deer in our forests were peering through the leaves toward the grasses, people of your color – or lack of color – came here. At first they seemed friendly, and, indeed, our own forebears took them for gods who had arrived from the fiery zone at the edges of the world from which the god of nature comes and goes at morning and at night. These people were the color of the stars and their attire gleamed. They claimed they were not gods but had a single God who had sent them. They planted a piece of cloth upon the beach and built walls and towers of native stone on a mountainside. And then, as the story goes, they killed our chiefs and made slaves of the rest of us. The God they called their own was cruel, not like our several gods who, in various places and at various moments of the great god's coming and going, provide us with what we need and warn us when storm is lurking on the edge of the world. The God of these people did not warn them, and one night our ancestors crept out of their shelters. We could blend into shadows. We were the color of the trees, even during the day. And so we are. We are of this place. Our gods were here before us. On that night, with the help of the goddess, who had darkened herself to a sliver in the lower sky, our forebears slipped on silent feet into the great stone place that these strangers had built and freed us of many of them. Their bones have long since been wound around by vines and have crumbled into the dirt. The others took themselves away in a great vessel."

"I understand from your story why you do not trust us," Estrella said.

The old man, cast his eyes around his people. Then he looked at the small and varied band from Archerland – Estrella's stalwart sons, Harry and George, Jerome the Gnome and his tall friend, the lissome Lisle, Tomaso, the moon-eyed Troll of the Bridge, Cybella and Grunius, Sheba and Blackie. Then, he looked at Estrella.

"No. We must learn that our first-sighting is not necessarily the truth. Your two animals could not accompany evil people. We will be friends."

Estrella held her arms out to her people.

"Rise. Come forward. Greet our friend, Umgalla, and his companions."

And they did.

"But now," Umgalla said, "something that you do not know. Others have come to inhabit those stones put on top of each other so many comings and goings of seasons ago."

"Others?" Estrella asked.

"Yes. And they are as evil as those who lived in that place once long before."

"What have you seen?" Estrella asked, trying to keep her voice calm lest she frighten her friends.

Umgalla described the Fortress and its inhabitants.

"And the leader is a tall, human-looking creature with a pearl-encrusted eye-patch?"

"Yes, you describe him perfectly."

"Mazlund!"

"And Vallarte must be with him!" Lisle said.

"Vallarte?" Jerome asked.

"He was my master when I lived in Corilus."

"We cannot escape Mazlund," Estrella said.

"So it seems!" Jerome said.

"Who is Mazlund?" Tomaso asked.

IV.

"But you are a princess of the realm!" said Gregg. "A Queen of Archerland!"

"Some princess! And Archerland is no more. The reports do not lie. I am still a woman," Glorimere said. "And no more than that."

"That may be, but I would find out otherwise, if..."

He paused.

"If what?"

"Were I to see you as a woman, no more than that."

"Your parents would object?"

Gregg laughed.

"No doubt they would!"

"Tell me about them."

"I am the last of their sons. My father left me his boat here in Stony Cove. My other brother lives in the city. He is a First Captain in the King's Fleet. My parents live in a cottage nearby."

"Then they could hardly object."

"I was thinking of your parents, Princess."

"My name is Glorimere."

"How well I know!"

Umgalla and Cybella spoke together at length about the song that his people sang.

"It is in the old language," Umgalla said. "We have never tried to place it in the words that you speak."

"I think I understand what you are saying though, from your gestures."

"Yes, almost every word in the old language has a sign. I have always thought that perhaps the signs came before the sounds."

"I think you are right. Or at least they were developed simultaneously."

Cybella arrived at this version of the ancient song.

"O, greatest god, god of the sky,
Look on us, great god of the sky,
Gaze upon us from up on high.

Open our streams from ice again,
Let them be free of ice again,
Let them melt again with rain.

And let our forest paths open,
Let snow melt and paths open,
So that we can hunt the game birds then.

Great god above, soften the earth,
Use your power to soften the earth,
So that our seeds can give their birth.

Let your warming arrive at last,
Let us below be warm at last,
Show us again that winter is past."

Umgalla was delighted with this translation.
"Call Majorum!"
She was Umgalla's granddaughter and a chief singer of the tribe.
"Teach Majorum the song, please," he said to Cybella.
And soon, once the tribe had heard Majorum's sweet voice ring the lyrics across the circle, they were all able to sing the song. They already knew the music.

Neutralon sat in the back of his small boat as the wave drew back and leaped forward again. He held on with both hands. The wave came down over the back of the boat, but did not crush it to the sand. Instead, he rushed toward the shore. He got out as the wave receded, pulling sand past his feet as he pulled his boat up to the beach by its painter. He stood for a moment and looked back at the waves marching in and calmly holding their breath until they came forward with a flash of fleece. It looked so peaceful, so orderly from the security of the land! Then he looked at the trees above the sand. The tapestry of branches and leaves gave way before his gaze. Yes! People there! And people he knew! Neutralon had been a solitary man, a prince isolated from the people who huddled below his towers in Enclava. But now he felt a yearning. He realized how lonely he had been for all these years.

Gradually, a plan began to form in Glorimere's mind. She had seldom ever planned anything. Her life had been set out for her, and her falling in love with Linvallen had hardly been part of the plan! But now, perhaps...

"Nothing keeps you here."

"I am a fisherman!"

She knew the fierce pride that these men of the sea had in their work. Gregg was no exception.

"I mean no family, no wife, no children."

"Those things, in time..."

"No doubt. But now is now!"

"I can't refute that."

"A storm is on the way," Harry said.

"I feel it too," Estrella said. "How do you know?"

"The birds are flying closer to the ground."

"How do they know?"

"Because the insects do. But don't ask me how they know! Perhaps they simply grow heavier with the moisture."

"How did you know about the birds?"

"Majorum told me."

"She did?"

"Yes. She and her people know these things. She can tell by the way a deer holds its head when the wind will change."

"I usually have to wait until the leaves turn white-side up."

"Yes. So do I. Grunius can read clouds."

"I know that," Estrella said.

"But he reads about some future event. The coming of an enemy. The arrival of a relief column. But Majorum and her people can predict the weather from the way the sky looks."

"Those high, wispy clouds usually come before a storm."

"Yes. We can tell some simple things. They can tell how long a storm will last, or how warm it will be, or how deep the snowfall will be.

They can make plans that way, plans for planting seed, plans for hunting, plans for taking shelter."

"They are wise in the ways of the land."

And you, my son, are learning to be that way too, she thought. And you are learning more than that.

Majorum was a lithe dancer and had a clear singing voice. She was also, like all of her small community, a skilled hunter and spear-fisherwoman. She also knew the ways of nature – how to read the leaves of an oak and find a spring nearby, how to listen to a stream and tell in which pool or eddy the trout might be hiding, how to pick up the fear that circulated through the woods from unseen animals when a predator approached who might be a danger to her – as opposed to just Majorum the hunter out for game for the evening meal. She knew that when deer turned to the left it was because they heard something. When they turned to the right it was because they saw something. In any event, they would quickly bound away on soundless hooves.

But for all of her wisdom, this was new, this young man with his pale skin – though it was turning brown in this outdoor environment – this feeling she had when he came near, this difficultly in breathing. But what was strange to her was that he did not mind learning from her, particularly how to read the signs that she picked up without a thought. She learned them again by giving words to them as she explained them to Harry. And he had one thing to teach her.

"Hold the stone between the thumb and forefinger."

"Like this?"

"Yes. Now tip your wrist back, keep your elbow close to your ribs and sling it."

"Like this?"

The stone curled over in the air and sliced into the pond with a slurp.

"You have to throw it so that it is parallel to the water."

She selected another stone from the shore.

"Like this?"

The stone skipped from circle to circle until it planed out of sight.

Majorum laughed.

"Yes," said Harry, "like that."

"You are still having difficulty?" Cybella asked.

"Yes. It is like trying to read a foreign language. And I mean one with strange letters to it. I can make out only the vaguest outlines."

"But they are better than nothing."

"Perhaps. But my gestalt might not be someone else's. So much rests in the interpretation of the shape."

"But yours is the experience."

"True. I am not sure how helpful experience is in this new world. I read the clouds and the horizon, particularly when seldom-seen stars are there below the trees. I can tell you this much. Whatever happens must happen before the new moon of summer, when the heat the earth has absorbed begins to pour out again."

"But how does that help us?"

"I know. We get no directive for action. Something will happen."

"But we do not make it happen."

"That would seem to be the conclusion."

"And that is not very helpful. It would seem that two competing theories of the future are colliding before your eyes."

"I sense that, yes. Whatever it is, it does signal caution," he said.

"I suppose it does. But, again..."

"Perhaps it means that we must not leap to conclusions."

"Yes. In other words, it may be something mental, not physical."

"I think so. I feel – though I cannot be specific – that we are at a kind of crossroads, but that we will only know what road we have taken when we are on it."

"I suppose that I can take that as optimistic," she said, laughing.

"It does depend upon the road. And, as I know, my Cybella, that is just a metaphor."

"And the future really has nothing with which to compare itself with."

"Not yet," he said.

"And I still dream of that wild place where I lived once now deep beneath the water."

"And do the dreams still trouble you?"

"Not as much. I recall the words of one of the chapters in that book of theirs – my favorite chapter – 'Much water cannot quench love, nor can the floods drown it.' That's from the Song of Solomon."

To Raise Another World

"That's my favorite chapter too!" said Grunius.

As the refugees began to breathe in their new atmosphere, the days and evenings provided an occasional space in which to think of the past. Estrella found the best moments to be just before dawn, when brief tremolo inquiries would invite full song into being, as if the fading stars had descended with a chorus into the trees. She thought of George, her husband. He had been the son of a devilish father and a mortal mother. She had seen the demonic in his eyes, as firelight touched their depths or as moonlight became their surface.

"I know it is there," he had said. "I can befriend that force. Those who do not know that it is there in them, who think themselves good, do evil. They do evil even as they prance around claiming to do the Lord's work, even claiming that they heard God's directive. The shadow of assumed benevolence is brutality. The dark side of sentimentality is a vicious disregard for all life."

For months, George, unable to gather the power to reform himself in human shape again, had served as a member of the Loyal Crow Brigade of Archerland. Then, one day he alighted upon a battle field in which many of Mazlund's Ungodly Guard lay dead. The grass was strewn with the half-uttered words of the charms with which these soldiers had tried to save themselves. George gathered the fragile sounds together by stroking his wing-feathers gently near the mouths of the fallen troopers and soon had enough to make his transformation into half-man again.

George could have made another choice as he lay dying on the battlefield. He could have uttered a magic word, "D'Nulzam!" and scuttled away as a rat or flopped away as a crow, healing his wound as he fled. This transformation he could have accomplished with a final pressure of human breath. But George had chosen the possibility of a human after-life, the possibility of seeing Estrella again. He had rejected the damnation that his demonic nature would have dictated. She knew that truth, and she continued to love him, as if his human form had not breathed its last on that long-ago field. But her own faith was failing her, had failed her. Would she be able to honor the rendezvous that he had picked out for them? A voice within her said no!

U.

Estrella waited in the grand audience chamber of Mazlund the Malign. She eyed the journals and paperbacks displayed on the table in Mazlund's opulent conversation area, where Chirac had seated her.

Creative Curses, Postmodern Maledictions, Making a New House Creak at Two AM, Ten Easy Steps to True Evil (Be Aware of Imitators), How to Be the Person You Never Could Be, Even If You Tried for the Rest of Your Life, Your Inner Monster, Sadists' Home Companion, and others.

"Ah Princess!" Mazlund said, entering the room. "Yes, my subscriptions have finally caught up with me. Or... should I say... Queen?"

"We have given up rank, here in Otherland," she replied.

"Otherland?"

"That is what we call it."

"I see. Well, that is easily negotiable. But you are here for the people, as their... ah representative?"

"I am."

"So you are their leader. I thought you had surrendered all hierarchy."

"We have. But we have not given up responsibility."

"No. Of course not."

"We still know what is right and what is wrong. A change in geography has not changed our nature. As the Prophet says, 'I will write my law in their hearts.'"

"Very good. I do enjoy theological debates! Your...ah... Princess Juna was so good at them."

"I cannot quote scripture as Juna could..."

Estrella had seen the stab of pain in Mazland's single eye as he had uttered her name. He looked almost human! But be aware of imitators.

Ah ha! Estrella thought. One of the disadvantages of being immortal! He lives on. People like Juna die. And Mazlund is left to mourn, but cannot say so. Were he a man, I would pity him. As it is, I do pity him for the eternity in which he must suffer.

"But," she said, "I learned from her the prophecy of Obadiah:

Though thou exalt thyself as the eagle
And though thou set thy nest among the stars
Thence I will bring thee down."

"Are you not afraid that the fate of the prophet will befall you?"

"I am no prophet, Mazlund. Prophets are either not believed or burned because they are believed."

"I mean the one who ignored the prohibition of the One Who Cannot Be Named?"

"The One Whom You Cannot Name, you mean. I assume that you refer to The Book of Kings? No. That prophet was killed by a lion, as was his donkey. But the lion ate neither prophet nor donkey."

"A lion? A scavenger worse than a hyena!"

"You know the story. The lion was the agent of – be ready to cringe, Mazlund — the Living Lord, not a hungry predator."

"But I forget myself! Wine?"

"I would enjoy a glass, thank you."

"Chirac!"

Chirac appeared, as if conjured up.

"Prince of Pickles?"

"Pickles?"

"The sour variety that make ones lips pucker in distaste."

"Oh, yes."

Mazlund had not heard that one. He was not sure he liked it, particularly when he was entertaining.

"What have you available from the cellar?"

"A crisp coviro blanco. A medium body chablis. A fruity coviro rosato. An exquisite Burgundy. A Pinot Grigio, fruity but agreeably dry. A chardonnay with a remarkable oaky intensity."

"I want to taste the wine, not the cask."

"Of course, Maestro of Mischief. A fresh Beaujolais, made from the fleshy Gamay grape, with a long, warm finish. A superb Silvaner, perfect with a lighter dish. A champagne that has been blended for years in its own chalk caves beneath an ancient city. It is round and harmonious. True Brut!"

"What will go well with fruit?"

"I suggest the Moscato, bottled at sea-level pressure but retaining a bubbly persona."

"Yes, bring us that," Mazlund said.

Estrella could tell that Mazlund was showing off. For her? She wondered why? Perhaps it was merely the reflex of a narcissist, enjoying this reflection of his success. He could have asked about the fruit first, after all.

"But to answer your question. No. I have not been forbidden to eat with you or to drink your wine."

Mazlund eyed her as he took a sip of his wine, a riesling with a dry sense of humor. Was it mocking him with its refreshing acidity? And how had she divined that he was wondering why she would share a glass of wine with him? The wine was part of the central ceremony of her misguided faith! Something to do with a table before my enemies?

"May I ask, Mazlund, why you have called this meeting?"

It had been merely to confirm his belief in her loss of belief, of course.

"I wanted to say that we can accommodate the presence of two different parties in this space. I see no conflicting agendas."

"What of the native inhabitants?"

"Oh them! We do not compete for the food supply – these woods and streams hold abundant game, deer and pheasant, and excellent trout, and the seas provide lobster and bluefish – and their primitive beliefs hardly conflict with ours. In fact, they are quite similar."

Yes, she thought. The natives believe in one great good. Mazlund is an adherent of one great evil. Each system had its totality. Her God included Mazlund within His scheme of things, because without an evil abroad no one could select the opposite. As long as Mazlund believed that the Living Lord had abandoned the pathetic group that had struggled out of the concentric circles that had finally closed over Archerland – or that they had abandoned their God – he would feel secure.

"And now," he continued, pouring more wine from his flagon into his glass, "you have given up your own silly superstitions. That desert whatever who so easily defeated Baal and Dagon and the other minor powers that stood in its way is no longer present to confuse you."

"That is true," she said.

But the truth was that Archerland had left the Living Lord and not the other way around. God had ceased to function because the inward nature of those who had been His people had grown neutral, or worse. Kermath had warned them.

"And I feel a great freedom!" she elaborated.

"Good! Good!"

Yes, she thought. You think that you now have a zone on which to work, having achieved this space in which to work. But her freedom, she knew, was her sense of release, the giving up of her individual power to that larger force that had touched her with sudden hope just as Mazlund made his statement about her loss of faith.

Chirac placed a bowl of grapes and cherries on the table on top of all the magazines.

"Some Moscato?"

"Thank you, no, Mazlund. I need to see with clear eyes."

"Of course you do. I hope you see what I see."

"I do."

"You do?"

"Yes. We pose no threat to each other."

"Ah... yes. That is true."

She had bought some time. They were outnumbered and certainly Mazlund enjoyed other physical superiorities as well. But he lacked the one thing he would always need, and he always would lack it. The Living Lord. Could she regain contact with that power again?

"We can be friends," he said.

"Of course. And you can help us."

"Tell me how?"

"We need some equipment. Pots and pans. Good bits for the horses that the natives have given us. Horseshoes. A few tools. We were able to salvage so little when we left. Scarcely ourselves!"

"Make a list. We will send those items with you as you leave. We are friends. We can share our good fortune."

"You are most generous, Mazlund."

His eyes glittered above his smile.

"Oh, and a workable spatula would be an uncovenanted blessing!"

He looked at her sharply, but she smiled back to signal her innocence of any irony.

We are no threat to him, she thought. Had he planned to attack us, he has canceled that possibility. Delayed it, at least. We have some time now to prepare, and to repair our long neglected relationship with the power that rules all things, visible and invisible, and who guides all creatures here below if they will listen. Even Mazlund. Particularly Mazlund! This man may be a narcissist, she thought. In fact, not being a man, he is the consummate narcissist. He imitates humanity so well! But regardless of his overweening self-esteem, he is not stupid. He is vain, but he knows how to resist an appeal to his vanity, primarily because he knows, deep-down, exactly who he is. And – who he is not. Still, I will insist that he show me his imitation of largesse.

"Ask and it shall be given," Mazlund said, still smiling, and pouring the last of his flagon into his crystal glass.

God works in mysterious ways, she thought, suppressing her strong desire to laugh out loud.

Mazlund gave the necessary orders.

"And two stout spatulas!" he said. "In case one should break or fall into the fire."

Yes, he thought. One of his problems in the past had been that Archerland believed in its supreme power. His mouth burned for a moment. He had come too close to naming it! But now, without that belief – and Estrella had confirmed its absence – the land was a free zone and subject to his own devices. The relationship between that 'whatever' and Archerland had been reciprocal. It required a returning response from its beneficiaries. Without that, it ceased to exist. Archerland's recent demise – not just its disappearance beneath the erasure of the waters, but its descent into civil war – had made the point.

But he recalled that he was host. This woman was, after all, his daughter-in-law, though he did not mention that. It was not a relationship likely to evoke her smile.

"You will stay for lunch? Of course. Chirac!"

Chirac was ready. His vocal training as an actor long ago came in handy at times like this, and his use of hand gestures to illustrate his words was eloquent in itself.

"A roast of corn-fed chicken with
a savory stuffing,
garnished with walnuts and with grapes,
and served with beans and with
tomato and roasted potato.

Grilled fillet of fresh salmon,
with lemon and herb-butter,
served with grilled tomato,
spinach, and new potato.

Baked sole (that's S O L E)
Served with a ragout of whole
potato, prepared with Tarragon
(fresh of course), leeks and chive.
A meal that is a milestone,
And for presentation – a perfect five!

Or as a light alternative,
a cold roast sirloin
of venison with salad
of tomato and cracked wheat."

He paused. Estrella politely clapped her hands.
"That was well done, Chirac! It all sounds so good!"
Chirac bowed then raised his palms as if to hold the applause.

"And for desert – a pudding,
served with dairy cream."

Estrella had the salmon, but skipped the pudding.

Mazlund escorted Estrella to the drawbridge, with a pony packed
with the goods she had ordered, He waved to her as she turned back
for a moment. Yes, he thought, I enjoy demonstrating my benevolence
to my subjects. And perhaps, on state occasions, Estrella will play the
hostess for me. Then he went to his own apartment and rang for Chirac.

"A bottle of your darkest port, Chirac. I am in the mood for a brief celebratory glass and then a well-deserved and, I hope, dream-free nap."

But, while Mazlund did sleep – his human shape demanded it – he dreamed of voices calling his name. And when he ran along those strange avenues that dreams open up to find the source of the voice, he could find nothing there at all. Yet still the voice was calling him. "Mazlund! Mazlund!" He awoke and saw a blanket of stars rolling down the horizon and into the woods outside his portal. Still half asleep, he said, "And once, I was one of them."

Now his single eye was wide awake. He had lost his other one when the lens designed to turn the castle of his opponents in Archerland to cinders had reversed its direction and attacked him. The eye was the one part of his being – whether as spider, crow, rat, or humanoid – that he could not reconstitute. That fact caused him to growl. And – oh yes – also incapable of regeneration was his soul. But that did not annoy him as much as did the partial physical blindness that interfered with his flying when he embraced his occasional crowhood.

VI.

Glorimere felt the spray from the sea sprinkle across her face and dry immediately as she stood on the bowsprit and stared at the horizon curling away under clouds in front of her. This was not like her first ocean trip, when she was off to Archerland escorted by the handsome Linvallen. But it was good. She was underway. She was no longer trapped in her stone cottage. She was no longer the object of scorn or pity. She was loved. And she loved.

"We are near where Archerland was," Gregg called to her from the helm.

Yes, they had looked at a chart together. Now, only the vastness of the waters spread over what had been the island kingdom of which she had been Queen.

She had persuaded Gregg easily enough, of course.

"Someone must have survived," she said. "They would have been blown eastward and found their way to land."

"I think that you are dreaming!"

"I do dream of that place. I do dream of those people. I must find them! I have no home here."

"And Archerland lies somewhere beneath the sea."

"But some of them..."

"We will see. No charts show anything beyond where Archerland was but ocean."

"Then we will find a new world!"

"Or merely an empty sea."

Lisle had been captured when she was a little girl by one of Mazlund's frequent occupations of Corilus, a city that had become his headquarters and the base for his many forays into the rest of Archerland. She had worked in the kitchens, first as a dough-carrier for the bakery, then as a serving girl for the voracious soldiers of

Mazlund's permanent garrison. She had grown dark-haired and comely, but had learned to hate the brutal soldiers on whom she waited. She became a favorite of Colonel Vallarte, one of Mazlund's cavalry commanders, but while her life became easier, her dislike of the regime and its soldiers and demonic beings deepened. She heard stories of another way of being and of a place called The Castle of Peace, where laughter and smiles were not a badge of cynicism. But she knew only one person from that world, Jerome the Gnome, who was Mazlund's spy.

Mazlund had promised Jerome that he could become a handsome hussar with decorations on his tunic, but Lisle had preferred the Gnome, who could tell her stories of this other place, with its sincere smiles and good-humored laughter. And Lisle knew that Jerome loved her, which is something she could not say of the suave Vallarte. And so when Lisle, floating in the sea after Archerland had disappeared into the mouth of the deep and had been picked up by the raft that carried Jerome and other survivors, she had been delighted. Shy at first, she soon realized that this group of refugees accepted her as one of them and did not condemn her for her unwilling association with the fortress at Corilus.

But one day, while she was getting water at the river below the encampment, she had been seized by one of Mazlund's scouting patrols. Soon, she was standing before Vallarte.

"So, you have returned to me!"

"I have been returned to you. I ask for my release. I am a free citizen of Otherland."

Vallarte laughed.

"Otherland! A place that does not exist! See that she is given a change of clothes. A bath first. Feed her. Then lock her in my chambers. Put a guard at the door."

A soldier thumped his chest and led Lisle away. And soon she was looking out at the distant smoke of what had been her encampment among the survivors of Archerland from the high, barred window of Vallarte's chamber.

A lean, sunburned man in a tattered cloak from which hung the remnants of gold braid and on the torn threads of cloth depictions of exotic birds and sinuous plants, approached Harry's post.

"Who goes?" Harry demanded, holding his spear toward the stranger.

"Prince Neutralon of Archerland."

Harry squinted at the man.

"Oh yes – I recognize you. Advance!"

Harry lowered his spear.

"How did you find us?"

"I came by boat, of course. Wind and current brought me here, as, I assume, it brought you."

"Yes. Come! We will go to the camp. The others will be happy to see you! Mazlund has come to these shores, and we need all the help we can get!"

"What?" Jerome asked.

"Lisle has been seized by one of Mazlund's patrols!"

This was spoken by Majorum, who had seen the encounter from a hillside and had watched as Lisle had been carried away on the back of one of the cavalry's chargers.

"You can do nothing," said Tomaso.

"But..." Jerome began.

"That building is impenetrable."

"But it isn't!" Grunius said.

"It's not?" Estrella asked.

"No. I have listened carefully to that Fortress. I can hear the footsteps of the guards," Grunius said. "One room exists above the moat that they seem not to know about. It exudes a serene silence compared to the angry whine of the rest of the place. And it can be reached."

"What then?" Tomaso asked.

"It's a start," Jerome said. "Getting inside the Fortress..."

"I'll go." Tomaso said.

"You?" Jerome exclaimed.

"Yes. I am small, and can conceal myself. Furthermore, I have some knowledge of the darker arts. You, Jerome, are too much involved in this. I can keep a cooler head as I find out where she is and decide how to free her."

"I doubt it," Jerome said.

"Ye of little faith," Tomaso said.

"You talk of faith?"

"I know my strengths."

"I know your limitations."

"But what choice do we have?" Estrella asked, breaking into the debate.

"None at all," Tomaso said.

And so, as shadows moved westward and surrounded Mazlund's Fearsome Fortress like a rising tide and as the first stars of evening began to try the eastern sky and as the moon began to send silver pathways along the forest floor again, Tomaso set out. He had had no chance to repay his friends of Archerland who had saved him from drowning. But in his heart he was hardly as confident as he had sounded when he had argued with Jerome earlier. Still, if he succeeded, he would have won a place among these people he so grudgingly loved. Or, as he himself knew, he could believe that he deserved that place. He could not hope for their love.

Mazlund stood on the parapet outside his Rooms of State, gazing eastward toward where Estrella was. He could see a trail of smoke rising from the further valley. It looked as if it were falling toward the fire, he thought, as if Icarus had plunged down to that spot, burning as he rushed into the friction of the atmosphere. He thought of the crucial moments of his interview with her. Oh, yes, he had pretended to be flattered into giving her some expendable items from the vast kitchen of the Fortress, but he had found out what he wanted to know. This place was his! And anything he gave to that ragged band would ultimately be his anyway. What does such generosity cost? He laughed. He recalled the look in her eyes.

"You have lost your faith in..."

He could not name it.

"... that power in which you believed."

And Mazlund was right! She had lost her faith in the Living Lord. How could He have permitted so many to perish as the waters lapped over the island like a thirsty tongue? How could He turn from the land on which He had bestowed such grace and which had returned that energy so fervently for so many years?

She had paused.

"That is right," she had said.

Mazlund rubbed his hands together.

But in her pause, Estrella had thought. Mazlund had summoned her for a conference and she had crossed the ponderous drawbridge under a white flag of truce.

What did he want? Obviously something advantageous to him, and that would mean that it would be bad for the survivors from Archerland who inhabited the western fringes of this continent. What Mazlund wanted, of course, was either to neutralize that small group or to destroy it. It posed a threat only if it retained its contact with that larger power that had so often defeated Mazlund in the past when he had seemed to have overwhelmingly superior forces at his command, and double their number in reserve. It had not all been bad luck or the incompetence of his commanders. No, Mazlund's lieutenants had been well-schooled in all that a modern army could accomplish in the field, march, countermarch, flanking action, repulse, defensive square, cavalry encirclement. And Mazlund's plans were invariably meticulous, formulated on detailed maps, accompanied by precise timetables, backed by contingency plans and the readiness of reinforcements to flow into line when needed. But he kept losing! What does Mazlund want me to say? Estrella wondered. He was clever, pretending not to be manipulative by his seeming directness, which was merely another element in the intricate fabric of his motivation.

At the moment that he made his statement, something had kindled in her. She had lost her faith, but as he made that claim for her, hope, even a touch of joy, had flowed back into her veins like the suffusion of a good wine, warming the blood, cheering the heart. But it was not physical. She remembered something Kermath, late counselor to the kings and queens of Archerland had said. "It is difficult sometimes for us to reach God. But it is easy for Him to reach us." And he had!

And so, Mazlund thought, I can act with impunity. I can show them whose flag flies over this land called TerraNova.

Mazlund did not object when told that his soldiers had captured Lisle. A show of strength. She had been a slave before. Slaves do not go around proclaiming their own freedom! It was a matter of the Ownership Society. Who owns whom, after all? And, once he had brought this paltry enemy under control – one by one, if necessary – and perhaps subdued the docile natives if he found it necessary, then he would prepare to confront his rival. Like the man long ago who had invented the lever, he had a place to stand! He would enjoy it for awhile before the final battle. He had fought once on the clouds, where the footing was slippery and where he had to keep using his wings to maintain his balance. And suddenly he had been propelled from that cumulous precipice with such force that he was barely able to recover to make a hard landing those countless fathoms down below. He had lost a lot of feathers and had suffered a sprained claw. But here on this ground he could win.

But as he went to bed the night after his meeting with Estrella, having consumed a brimmer of wine and finding that his head spun within a zodiac of bright lights when he closed his eye, he heard an old, familiar voice.

> "You, Mazlund, your former name is lost
> in time, in time before the time began
> and suns rose and then the moonlight ran
> to pave the sky for stars. For when you crossed
> the power you cannot bring yourself to say,
> you doomed yourself to live a spider's life,
> to scuttle like a rat, and for a day
> to feel as humans do, without belief,
> giving you only everlasting pain
> knowing that peace will never come again
> to a soul in flames, like those that gathered round
> you as from heaven high you tumbled down.
> And now, in your rage, you can only try
> to make others suffer. But you cannot die."

He got up in the night and stared from his portal at that place where a pale vestige of campfire etched itself into the predawn blackness.

Harry and Majorum were having a rock-skipping contest – number of skips counting equally with the length of the total individual skip, divided by the number of failures, which were very few. Sheba was with them.

"No, Sheba!"

"She thinks she can catch the stones before they sink," Majorum said.

Harry picked up a stick.

"Here, Sheba!"

He slung the stick into the pond. Sheba leaped in with an explosion of water and brought the stick back to Harry.

"Now," he laughed, "we will be here all day!"

But they finally placated a panting Sheba. They sat under an oak tree and watched the light on the water.

"Do you know what those cleared spaces are at the bottom?" she asked.

"No."

"Fish clear them with their tails, so they can lay eggs there."

A breeze came up. Rain seemed to fall from the clear sky.

"From the leaves," she said. "The after-rain."

Tomaso slipped under the shadow of the drawbridge, getting a sudden whiff of homesickness as he sniffed the damp wood. He had lived under damp wood for most of his life! He paddled down the moat, keeping to the shadows and the eddies near the Fortress walls, until he came to the ladder, pocked with rust where it was not thick with moss. Up he went, pulling with his arms and pushing with his legs, since the ladder had not been designed with trolls in mind. Flakes of rust and clumps of moss dropped behind him, softly into the water. He entered the chamber.

Now what? he asked himself.

He had better ask.

He slipped into a corridor and tiptoed toward a guard post – an archway recessed into the stone walls. He slipped behind the guard, who was leaning against his spear, half-asleep.

Another guard approached.

"Anything?"

"Not even a mouse."

"Your relief will be along at midnight."

The first guard heard himself asking a question.

"Where are they keeping the new princess?"

The first guard spun around but could see nothing in the shadows behind him. Tomaso had lived in shadows for most of his life and had learned their ways. They expanded or shrunk according to the light. He could sense how much light existed in any given place and fit himself into whatever shadows were lurking nearby. These corridors were easy!

"In Vallarte's quarters, of course," the second guard replied. "North side. Why do you ask?"

The first guard thought it best to pretend that he had asked.

"Just curious."

"Be curious about what a guard should be curious about! Curiosity killed the frog!"

"Yes, sir!" But it had not been the frog. He had been a prince in disguise!

"She's hardly a princess," the second guard muttered, continuing down the corridor.

Tomaso scuttled away, shorter than the shadows that concealed him.

"I am not doing enough," Grunius said.

"Of course you are!"

"What am I doing, Cybella? Here Tomaso goes off in search of Lisle!"

"You are reading horizons, clouds, and stars."

"Yes, but this is an every day situation of ours. We live in a world of present necessity, not one that can ease toward some future to be discerned in the hieroglyphics of trees against a sunset, or the shaping of cumulous, or the way the zodiac is angled on a summer's night."

"But we do concern ourselves with the future. We store food. We fill the cracks in our shelters against the chilly fingers of the storm. We gather wood and pile it nearby. Not too near, of course."

"No. Ants. But that again is practicality. I am a theorist. A dreamer. I am a builder of castles in the air. I have no place in this society based on the rigor of fact alone."

"But we still need to know more. You have told us that we must beware the moment when the earth begins to give up its stored heat."

"Yes, when that heat goes outward it sets fire to part of the sky and meteors shower back toward us. But what that means I do not know."

"It means that we exercise caution."

"We do anyway," he said.

"But we could grow careless."

"We have," he said. "I saw nothing that would warn Lisle."

A cloud lumbered like a man-of-war across the sun. He looked up.

"You!" he said.

"Me?"

Grunius trembled for a moment.

"Yes. You be cautious."

"Even before the summer's flow of upward heat?"

"Yes. For my sake."

"I will," she said, laughing, "since you put it that way!"

But her laughter was a cover for her reaction to the whiteness that had dwelt on Grunius's face for an instant.

"It is Harry! Quickly!"

"What happened, Majorum?" Estrella said, following the girl from the encampment.

"Stung by a wasp!"

"But a wasp..." Estrella said, catching up to the running girl.

"I know! I have sent for Releah!"

Harry was lying in a leafy glade. Estrella knelt down and touched his forehead. It was hot. Harry was gasping, as if he could barely pull any air over his lungs. His face was swollen.

"A wasp did this?" she asked.

"It all happened so quickly," Majorum said. "But I heard him make a sound of pain and saw the wasp fly away. Then he fell."

Releah came into the circle.

"Majorum told me what happened," she said.

"Can you do anything?" Estrella asked.

"I am not sure," Releah said, looking gravely at the young man struggling for breath on the leaves.

Blackie was, as cats can be, adept at slipping into and out of places where he could find food. But not just any food. Blackie, as cats can be, was an epicure. He did not mind munching on mice, but he preferred the finest of fish, and he could sniff out the finest of fish even if the remnants were miles away. He enjoyed licking at the bones of the trout that his own family cast aside, but he liked even more the delicate leftovers of the Mazlundian feasts of the Fortress. Since the drawbridge was seldom up, Blackie could slip like the night across to the keep and slither along the shadows to the doorway to the refectory. An easy leap to a jutting buttress, a further jump to the stone window above the door, which was always open, a pounce to a table below, and he was there. The cook would be scraping the remains of a salmon repast into a refuse bin. And soon Blackie would be inside that bin, savoring the delectable leftovers and saving the trashman a fraction of his labors. Blackie would return to his camp, and Sheba would turn up his nose. Where have you been?

One evening, as Mazlund made his way from his Executive Dining Room, contented with a meal of venison, sluiced down with a velvety Burgundy with that long finish that only the finest vineyards could provide, and feeling almost human, a black cat shot across his path. Blast! The problem with this human shape! Why do I get this feeling of foreboding just because a harmless cat has intersected my path at a right angle? But Blackie turned and licked a paw, as if mocking Mazlund, and let his yellow eyes pick up the torchlight and flick it across what had been a satisfied smile. Mazlund hissed at the cat, and it sauntered casually out of sight. I am glad I am not hiding out as a rat, Mazlund thought. I did not like the way that cat looked at me!

VII.

Gregg tacked back and forth to the lee side of the cape and brought the boat toward the shore.

"If any of your friends survived, this is where they would be."

"I hope so."

But she had a sudden fear. Not everyone at Archerland had been her friend. And many who seemed to be had no choice. She had been a Queen! And she had betrayed King Mark. She had caused a civil war, the news of which reached Leatops at almost the same time as did the tidings of Archerland's erasure from all maps. If she found someone she had known in that former life, would she be welcome? Or reviled? She felt that to be hated was what she deserved. But that response, she recognized, might result from the hatred she felt for herself at times. Even Gregg's love could not always erase that self-hatred. I deserve it, she thought. I do not deserve his love.

"Perhaps they have already watched our approach," Gregg said, sensing her sudden doubt.

"I'm not sure," Glorimere said, as if to herself.

Gregg released the mainsheet. The sail dropped, like a cloud suddenly cleaved by the wind. He went forward and held the anchor in both hands. He was ready to toss it into the sand as soon as the boat slowed. He and Glorimere would row ashore in the dingy. He, too, was not sure, but he was sure that his uncertainties were not the same as Glorimere's.

"Yes, he was stung on the arm."

Releah dipped a cloth into a bowl, turning the cloth around and around until no liquid remained in the bowl and placed the cloth above the red circle with the white center on Harry's arm. She held it there with the fingers of her right hand.

Estrella rinsed another cloth in water and wiped Harry's face.

"Yes," said Releah. "We must get the heat out of his body. We need just the right amount in our bodies. Too little, or too much..."

She did not complete the sentence.

"But could a wasp...?" Estrella asked.

"Yes," said Releah. Her wrinkled old face drifted toward thought as she held the cloth against the site of the sting.

"The wasp can poison a person. It is rare, but I have seen it happen."

"And...?" Estrella could not complete her question.

"It is possible," the old woman said. "Majorum came to me quickly. And she told me what had happened, so that I was able to prepare these herbs without delay."

"What do they do?"

"They draw the poison out through the pathway of its entrance. The question is whether we can reverse the flow."

"And...?"

"Put the cool cloth behind his neck."

They waited. Nothing seemed to change.

"Shouldn't your medicine be taking effect?" Estrella asked.

"Listen!" Releah said.

They did.

Majorum had said nothing for quite a while, merely rinsing off fresh cloths to hand to Estrella. It was a mother's task, she knew, to soothe the forehead of her son.

"Yes!" Majorum said. "He's breathing!"

The gasping had eased and now Harry was taking long breaths, as if to compensate for the air he had not been able to get to his lungs. The swelling around his eyes was diminishing.

"His brow is cooler!" Estrella said.

"Yes, the poison is leaving him," Releah said quietly, as if that were no surprise to her.

"Bless you!" Estrella said.

Releah smiled and pointed at the patch of sky above the oak tree beneath which Harry rested.

Lisle had given up hope. Here she was, once more trapped within the walls of a dispensation she despised, prisoner of the odious Vallarte, a man who thought himself instantly beloved of all who cast eyes upon him. He had never met a mirror he did not like. But, she thought, I have no choice. And Vallarte would be back from patrol soon.

Well, she would have some wine and be at least numb by the time he returned.

"Lisle!"

She turned, spilling some wine on her hand. Her name had come from the shadows of the far wall of the chamber.

"Come! No time to lose!"

"Tomaso?"

"Yes. Follow me. I will imitate the captain of the guard as we go. As each guard goes down the corridor, hide in his post. We will keep doing this until we get to the east side of the Fortress. Can you swim?"

"Swim?"

"Pull yourself thorough the water with your arms and legs?"

"No."

"I hope you are a quick learner," Tomaso said. "Come!"

"No. I dreamed."

"Do you remember?"

Back among the living, Harry looked at Majorum. A wrinkle of concern still played along her brow.

Harry had experienced utter blackness, deeper than the busy gray that he saw when he closed his eyes. And silence absolute. He became aware that what he knew as silence was really a constant buzzing of life, almost like the whine of the wasp just before it had stung him.

Then a gradual light began to flow behind each eye in two separate paths. Then the paths joined. It was made of light and had only darkness as its boundary. It would not hold his weight, he thought, even as it did. And so he walked for what seemed like a long time. The path became a circle. And in that circle he saw voices. He did see them even if they were like clouds, or fragments of smoke, and on them were words that he could hear. Or rather, they became the words, fluidly weaving around the circle.

"You are not to come here. You are to return. We send you back with love. Time enough will exist for your stay with us. But that time is not yet."

And he knew who had spoken in that misty language, that phrasing of vapor that somehow he had heard. It had been Killbeard, and

Evalinda, and the two kings named Paul, and the Princess Juna, and Kermath, and his father Mark, and even Linvallen, who had fought his father on the shores in that final battle. All of them had spoken in his or her single voice, yet the voices had been blended into that swirl of light that had moved around the island, as if the luminous language had been prepared for him as he stood there looking across at them. Yes, he realized that he had been looking across, but he did not know what had separated him from the imagery of the voices.

"And you are back," Majorum said.

"Yes," he said, reaching up to touch the tear on her cheek.

He placed his finger against his tongue.

"And I am hungry!" he said.

"You will be fed," she said.

He noticed the crinkle of concern that remained in her brow. Perhaps for him. Or something else?

She would soon have to tell him that Lisle had been captured by Mazlund. Does no joy come, she wondered, without a shadow?

"Hello there!"

"Who goes?" Harry called.

"My name is Glorimere."

"Glorimere?"

"Yes. And I have Gregg with me."

"Is this the Glorimere who was Queen of Archerland?"

It would be foolish to deny it.

"Yes."

"Advance!"

She and Gregg approached the sentry post.

"Harry!"

"Welcome, Glorimere! Welcome – was it Gregg?"

"I am so happy to have found you!" Glorimere said. "How many Archerlanders are there here?"

"Come! You will meet them. They will be happy to greet you again, and your friend, Gregg."

They will? she wondered.

But they were. She entered the quivering warmth of the campfire, with the faces, bright and shadowed, circling around it.

"Glorimere! Welcome!" Estrella said. "And your friend! Gregg, is it? Come! You must be hungry after your journey. Join us. We have plenty."

Those around the fire widened their circle. Glorimere, with a tentative smile, joined them, Gregg by her side.

"Gregg is a fisherman," she said. "His boat is in the cove."

"Good," said George. "I catch fish down in the stream. I want to learn how to fish from a boat."

"I will teach you," Gregg said.

"Grunius, extra plates!" Cybella called.

"So I see," Grunius replied. "Welcome, Glorimere. Welcome, Glorimere's friend."

Tomaso had lived among echoes all his life, and he knew their ways.

And, as with shadows, these corridors were easy.

"Report to the Captain of the Guard!"

This command ran down the corridor to each post, and each sentry came fully awake, pulled himself from his leaning posture on his spear and rushed off toward the Central Command Post. Tomaso and Lisle followed. The only tricky part was when each guard, having been reprimanded by the Captain for leaving his post, came back down the corridors. Tomaso and Lisle hid.

"Report to Vallarte immediately!"

The Captain of the Guard looked for the source of the voice, saw no one, but thumped his chest and rushed past them on the way to Vallarte's quarters. He did not know that he was anticipating Vallarte's command, soon to be given in emergency-mode, which meant an angry shout wrapped like a sandwich in imprecations that made the ancient stone walls blush.

"Now," said Tomaso, having demonstrated the technique of the dog-paddle, saving the crawl and the side-stroke for later lessons, "whatever you do, don't stop. Keep your arms moving and your legs kicking. If you cannot keep it up, roll over onto your back. You will float, and I will pull you along. We only have to get to the bridge. Then we can climb up to the path on the other side and be on our way!"

All was going well, Lisle actually enjoying her newfound ability to keep her head above the dark waters of the moat, until they heard shouting and saw the bridge begin to rise. Vallarte had given the alarm and now a band of moonlight ran across the moat where the bridge had been and up the wall where the handholds were that would have brought Tomaso and Lisle to the road under cover of the bridge.

On the night in which Glorimere arrived, Neutralon told his story, which paralleled the narratives of the other survivors. Natural forces had destroyed Archerland, but those same forces had brought them to these shores.

"The prevailing easterlies," Gregg said. "They brought us here as well."

Gregg smiled at Glorimere. She smiled back, relieved that Neutralon's narrative made it possible for her to avoid her own. She had been a traitor to Archerland!

"Yes," said Neutralon, "and the good fortune of surviving when my tiny boat capsized in the surf."

"That, plus all those fish you ate."

"True. I don't suppose..."

"No fish tonight," Grunius called. "We have venison stew just coming to a simmer." Grunius's duties included those of cook for the encampment. Soon, he hoped, once their civilization took hold, he could promote himself to chef. He did enjoy the satisfied smiles he received when his various concoctions were sampled. He had discovered, as many cooks do, that he had an instinctive sense of how much or how little of this or that turned out to be, in the opinion of his cliental just right. "A dash of dill," he would say when asked for his secret. He did not use the French word that he had learned from Mazlund, primarily because he did not know how to spell it. Grunius still wished he could do more for his colleagues.

"Good!" said Neutralon. "I need a change of cuisine!"

As Grunius handed Neutralon one of the bone-china plates that Estrella had been given by Mazlund, she told Neutralon that Mazlund had established himself nearby.

"Inevitably," he said. "And, by the way, this is excellent stew! It is not just that I have longed for such a dish. A soupcon of oregano perhaps?"

"You have a well-tuned palate!" Grunius said.

"We need guidance," Estrella said.

Neutralon looked at the crepuscular sky.

"We have received no sign," said Estrella.

"If not from above..." Neutralon said.

"Yes," Estrella responded, picking up his thought. "In the past, we have gone to our ancestors, sought out their perspective, asked them where we are placed and to what position we may be moving within the framework of eternity."

"Within that segment of eternity that includes human history," Neutralon said. "And you yourself have made such a journey."

"True, although the words I brought back were not helpful to King Mark."

She saw the sudden pain on Glorimere's face.

"Oh, it was already too late, Glorimere. The King had already decided on civil war."

"But if I..."

"We can relive past history only if we learn from it," Grunius said. "That much I learned from Kermath. If we live the past only as pain we do what the damned must do. But we still have a choice."

"Perhaps we do get a sign now and then," Glorimere said.

"I wish we would!" Estrella replied.

"I dreamed last night, as we rode at anchor, of a great castle, walled and with a gigantic keep, a moat formed by a river around it, and a heavy portcullis of intricately wrought iron above the drawbridge," Glorimere said.

"Mazlund's Fortress!" Estella exclaimed.

"Is it? Deep within the place I dreamed is a door," said Glorimere. "At least it was so in my dream."

"An opening into the ancestral mind, perhaps," Grunius said.

"That could be," Glorimere said. "I had the feeling that something important lay behind that door."

"I want to have a look at this Fortress of his," Neutralon said.

Jerome had learned the technique from his friend, Umgalla.

"Lisle likes mushrooms," Jerome had said.

"Yes, the way to many a woman's heart!"

"But I am no hunter-gatherer."

"True, you are a creature of the court."

"I am?"

"Oh yes. You are diminutive, but elegant. Your disqualifications notwithstanding, I will teach you how to find mushrooms."

And so Jerome learned that moss likes moisture and darkness and is therefore to be found on the northside of trees, where the sun seldom shone with its dry beams.

"And, if you pursue that shadow outward for a few paces and look to left and right, as the shadow moves with the seasons, you very are likely to find mushrooms."

And so Jerome became the colony's hunter of mushrooms. He also found wild berries. He also found an edible blackish fruit that Lisle called a truffle. Jerome began to contribute to the economy of the Archerland survivors, even in the category of luxury foods. Still, he thought, here in this desert place, we need our moments of pleasure. The survivors began to look forward to his return from the woods. Invariably he brought something that would add to their meal, turning it into a feast.

Umgalla looked at Estrella.

"Your son, Harry, and my daughter, Majorum, have become friends."

"Yes!"

"And you do not object?"

"Object? No. Do you?"

"No. Your son is an excellent young man. He is quickly learning the ways of the forest."

"Yes, and your excellent young daughter is teaching him. We have embraced this new world, Umgalla. We must learn to live in it and with it. We are not so foolish to believe that we can impose our will upon it. We would be disappointed."

"Yes, as were the metal-clothed conquerors of my ancestor's time."

"They left without their gold. We did not come here seeking gold."

"I thought I should tell you..."

"What I already know. But thank you."

A log tumbled into the fire, sending an explosion of blue-green across Umgalla's face.

"And they took the cruel principle they called God with them," Umgalla said.

"Yes. I understand your suspicion of us. I cannot blame anyone for calling that kind of power sadistic, and the people who worship it as masochists. But we believe in a more loving deity."

At least I think we do, she said to herself. The survivors of Archerland seemed to have arrived at a place closer to Umgalla's version of higher power than the one that had presided over the sunken kingdom. Or, she amended, that many of us believed in once upon that long ago.

"So I see," said Umgalla.

But what did he see? she wondered.

"Another thing," Umgalla continued, "of a possibly more immediate nature. We cannot stand neutral in the face of Mazlund. He is a threat to you."

"I know. And I thank you again. But we do not know what he intends."

"He means no good."

"Yes, that much we know. But he has grown devious. Once he believed that he could sweep our small army from the field with a mere glance of his cavalry. He gradually learned that he could not. Even evil has its evolutionary process."

"Except perhaps that it never learns one thing."

"Right, Umgalla. That it can never succeed. Although..."

"No, the loss of your kingdom, as you describe it, was a natural event."

"But the Living Lord..."

"As you tell your story, your people had turned away from your God. That meant that nature was free to work its will – and it has a will of its own – and that you would not be warned. Therefore, the natural event could not be part of the design of any God. You have told me that your God warned of the flood."

"Yes. He selected a righteous man called Noah and told him to prepare for waters that would rise to the mountain tops."

"You see?"

"I think so. It was a rainbow that saved us once. It attached itself to the island on which Mazlund had established his dominion and pulled the island back to the main."

"And then you were still combating evil."

"Yes."

"And you are again, regardless of whether you sense the hand of your God in your everyday activities."

"And you will stand with us?"

"Of course. And we need no treaty, just as we need no maps. We know where things are. For what it is worth – a frail force of hunters with bows and arrows designed for the shortest of ranges – we will stand with you."

"That will help us."

"Perhaps. I believe that it will help us. We would like to align ourselves with whatever larger power lies behind the natural world. In the latter we do believe, of course."

"You have lived within its power for all these years."

"For generations that are beyond our ability to count. But that there may be something more? We can only find out by standing with you. We would betray our own nature were we to stand aside."

Cybella was up before dawn, wandering a meadow as stars eased from the skies. When she returned, she described her adventure to a sleepy Grunius.

"The moon was at its most slender – merely a finger nail as it touches through the Pleiades. But as it came to the horizon in the northeast, stars were washed away, and the earthshine just before dawn created the moon, full-circle."

"The dark part?"

"Yes, just for an instant. I was looking at something that was there and wasn't there."

"Yes! You saw both the past and the future in the outline."

"True – the planet as it has been and will be. But more than that."

"Yes – but what?"

"Something that is there and isn't there."

"Like the future."

"Yes. But it often takes the future to tell us what it is."

"How well I know!" said Grunius. "How often have I said to myself, 'Why didn't I see that at the time? It was so clear!'"

"Clarity is in retrospect."

"Not always."

"Let's hope not!" Cybella said.

Tomaso himself was getting tired. His stumpy arms and chunky legs were not suited for marathons.

"Come!"

He and Lisle held on to the rugged stones in a shadow on the side of the moat.

"How are you holding up?"

Lisle took a deep breath.

"I am all right. But getting cold."

The draw bridge thumped into the wall of the Fortress and the portcullis dropped in front of it with clang that made the moat tremble.

"Yes. We are going to have to swim under where the bridge was. There's a low point on the south side of the castle, a kind of beach."

"Is it guarded?"

"Probably. I suppose we will have to find out."

His voice conveyed their lack of any other choice. He did not tell her that he had noticed the snouts of two crocodiles, eyes looking at them, in the glitter of water behind them.

Down stream they went, their movements getting spasmodic in the cold water. But the current was strong, and soon they were lying on the mud bank that Tomaso had described.

"Let's crawl up just a little higher," he said.

A bell rang from the Fortress, echoing within the courtyard and sending rings of alarm across the darkness beyond the walls.

"What is that?" asked a guard nearby.

"Let's find out!" said the other guard.

They rustled away in the darkness, their torches making momentary monsters of the trees.

"Come!" said Tomaso. "The southern road is close by. It will curl around to the hillside where our camp awaits us!"

Lisle had no breath with which to reply. But she rose and followed Tomaso toward the gleam of roadway that the moon opened out before them.

"Lisle!" Jerome shouted and shuffled across to her.

"Why yes. I can swim like a duck, did you know that? Tomaso taught me how."

"A crash course," Tomaso said.

He looked around. Every face was on him, most looking down, of course, because of his markedly less than middle height. But there on a level with his were the eyes of Jerome, and below them a smile.

"I am your friend forever," Jerome said.

"I am glad," Tomaso said. "Much more unites us than divides us."

"And that is true for all of us," Estrella said. "And that embrace includes our newer friends, the people of Umgalla, who have made us welcome on these shores."

VIII.

On the day after his arrival, still savoring the breakfast of pheasant eggs Grunius had prepared for him, Neutralon looked across the valley toward Mazlund's Fortress.

"What do you see?" Grunius asked.

Neutralon once had a tapestry that showed an area around his castle in Enclava more vast than the eye could see from his parapets even on a clear day. The tapestry could also depict future events. Neutralon had seen himself led from prison toward the gallows one chilly morning. And that had been accurate. Fortunately, the progress of his execution had been interrupted at, literally, the last minute, just as the clock on the tower of the Old Kirk had been inhaling for its announcement. Before Archerland had been gulped up by the ocean's mouth, the tapestry had shown the land to be under water, familiar pathways writhing in weeds. Neutralon had to leave his tapestry behind, but he discovered that years of looking at that tapestry had given him the ability to see more than other people could. Not, he knew, to see more than the eye could take in, but to sense something beyond what he saw. The power was something similar to what people called insight. His specific version was linked, as the tapestry had been, to the future.

"A door does exist," Neutralon said. "Deep within that Fortress."

"Well and good," Grunius said. "What do we do about it?"

"I think I know," Neutralon replied.

"Crocodiles?" Grunius asked.

"Yes. In the moat," Lisle said.

"They were left over from the false world I tried to make for Mazlund. Perfectly harmless. They are scared of haddock!"

"Yes. I thought the water was too cold for real crocodiles."

"Did Tomaso see them?"

"No. I didn't tell him. He was having a hard enough time just keeping his head above water!"

60

Cybella shook free of the grasp of two of Mazlund's Terror Troopers.

"I can walk by myself."

"Just don't try anything."

They were almost out of the small grove of trees in front of the drawbridge of the New Fortress of Fear, as Mazlund had named it.

I must escape before we enter those walls, Cybella thought. But how?

Cybella felt something. Yes – a call coming toward her from the side of the path.

She paused.

"Keep going!" shouted one of the soldiers.

But she darted to the side of the path and disappeared.

"Where'd she go?"

"Hiding among these trees."

"Let's burn them down."

"But our master will want her alive."

"No. One less enemy. One less prisoner to worry about. Escape attempts. Rescue efforts. Hunger strikes. The depressing effects of execution on our men."

And soon the soldiers had set fire to the dry leaves that had been gathering on top of each other for generations beneath the oak of the woods. A sigh went up from the trees.

A soldier coughed as a puff of acid smoke smote him in the face.

"Let's get out of here!"

The flames were leaping now, beginning to lick at the thick trunks of the trees that had produced the fuel for the fire.

"When we press upon the ground and it still oozes with water, that means that ice still rides just below the surface. When the ground no longer oozes, the water is below, waiting for the seed. Such things are simple. I am surprised you do not know them!" Majorum said.

"There is much I do not know," said Harry.

"Faces, for example," she said.

"Faces?" Harry asked.

"Yes. In that cloud. It is a frown."

"Does that mean a storm?"

"Yes. It usually does. And the storm means more faces."

"Where?"

"Where it is warm, of course. Where the fire is."

"And you see faces there?"

"Of course. And they also tell their stories. They tell of after the storm."

"You will have to teach me the language."

"Of cloud and flame?"

"Yes. So much I do not know!"

"That is why we look for those faces and listen for their stories. They see more than we do, if they are clouds."

"Of course. And fire?"

"Fire lives very quickly, so that its stories are like a dream. A lifetime seems to pass as we listen, even if only a few moments have really gone by."

"And so you take that lifetime into your moment?"

"Yes! You are learning! The fire tells you that your own life is but one of many and that your own life includes the life that has been..."

"And the life that is to be."

"Ah yes," said Majorum, laughing. "As were our ancestors, we are here for the life that is to be."

"Watch!" Majorum cried.

She picked up a stone and tossed it into the calm waters of the bay.

Harry saw a school of fish suddenly illuminated by the sun coming over the trees and shining into the water. The fish were many, silver and swift as they fled the stone that had been tossed in front of them.

"How did you know they were there?"

"Oh, I could see them," Majorum said. "They are grey and shrugging, like the waves. But they were not going in that direction. I wanted you to see them."

"Thank you. They hide from the sun."

"Yes. They chase other fish that hide from the sun. And, of course, other fish chase them."

"Hide and seek."

"Yes, like that game you told me of. Under the ocean's surface it is a constant game of hide and seek."

"And the loser is swallowed up."

"Nature's way," she said.

"Yes. And Mazlund has us playing his game as well."

She looked over her shoulder at the forest behind her.

"Yes, and even now one of his people has eyes upon us."

"How do you know?"

"Just as I can see the fish moving like the water but not in the direction of the waves, I can sense a disturbance in the trees. The animals there have moved away from something that does not belong there."

"Cybella has been captured!"

Jerome rushed into the camp on his stunted legs, pointing back toward the valley.

"By whom?"

"A squad of Mazlund's, patrolling the woods near the fortress."

"What were you doing there?"

"We were scouting out weak spots."

"Yes," said Grunius, "and they came up behind you."

"That's what happened."

"But you got away."

"I don't think they saw me. I was lower than the bushes from which we were peering at the place. But they grabbed her by the shoulders."

"Show me where."

"That will do no good."

"It may. She has powers."

"The boat sure stinks!" George said, laughing.

"It does," Gregg agreed. "Fish scales, old bait, rotten rope. Some things have gathered in the hold for years. And even if they are not there now, they have left their memory!"

"Show me how you find the wind."

"Look at the water. See that calm place, clear as a pane of glass?"

"Yes."

"To the left the water is much busier. In which direction is that water moving?"

George stared from the stern, where he sat, the tiller of Gregg's boat under his right arm.

"It's moving toward that calm sector."

"That's right. And that's where the wind will be when we get there. Steer to the left about ten degrees."

George did so.

"And be ready to haul on the mainsheet!"

And soon the boat was spanking across the waters. George laughed.

"Great! What fun!"

"Yes," Gregg said. "It can be. The motion of the boat and its coming to life as something invisible fills the sails can be enjoyable. It makes up for the work that you can still smell in the hold."

He held up his right hand, callused and torn and healed.

"And the hauling of nets."

"Yes," George said. "I am learning that much as well. And the pain at the base of the spine."

"Yes," Gregg said, laughing. "But with you as my helper, we are supplying our company with white fish and those gigantic crabs and the black lobsters that turn red in those pots that Mazlund so kindly gave to your mother."

"Just think," George said, "if Archerland had not sunk beneath the ocean, I would never have learned to be a fisherman!"

"That's true," said Gregg. "I am very happy to be a fisherman again. Some are born to it. And those that are will never be happy doing something else."

"I don't think I would be either. But I enjoy finding the wind more than hauling the nets."

"No one will blame you for that preference. But now, young sir, it is time to pull up the wooden traps we have set on the ledges to find what harvest they will yield for our feast tonight."

"I know that they will yield me a pain at the base of my spine!"

"Smoke!" Grunius shouted.

He rushed ahead of the twisting gait of the Gnome.

The floor of the forest was on fire. Grunius put his nose in an elbow and rushed into the grove.

He almost turned back as the heat pulsed against his forehead, but he saw the end of the path ahead through a liquid tapestry of flame and skeletal leaves and the luminous whiteness that fire gives off. And, yes!

"Come from the tree!" he commanded, holding his arms out, then coughing.

"Come, I charge thee!"

And Cybella was before him, grabbing his hand and pulling him toward the air at the end of the pathway. They fell gasping, just beyond the grove.

But the drawbridge a few yards away rumbled with the thunder of an out-going patrol.

"Quickly!"

Cybella pulled Grunius to his feet. They ran toward the moat that surrounded the Fortress and jumped in. Keeping to a shadow on the western side of the wall, they came to a moss-encrusted ladder that lead to a small balcony.

The sounds of the search echoed around them, as if the voices were coming from the dark waters of the moat.

"They won't look for us inside the castle," Cybella said.

"Yes," Grunius said. "Sometimes you have to go in an unexpected direction."

And so, shivering from the water in the coolness of twilight, they crept into that evil-free room in the fortress that had seldom felt a footstep in three hundred years.

"I'm cold," said Grunius.

"One extreme to another," Cybella said.

"And hungry."

"We will be hungry and no doubt suffer from sniffles," she said. "But this is a good place to know about. It will help Neutralon as well."

She paused.

"What's wrong?" Grunius asked.

"My friend, Simeon the Oak. He sheltered me. And he was burned, ring by ring, for helping me."

"We lose our friends in these battles," Grunius said, knowing that his words could do little good.

"Too many. I sometimes wonder whether we just fight on because of our desire for revenge."

"That's a motive, true. But Mazlund is evil."

"Does that make us good, when our friends die like that?"

"Not necessarily. But it does tell us why we fight."

And later that night, just as the moon set, and the chill made guards lower their heads to think of hearths in warm halls and cups of wine, Cybella and Grunius slipped down the mossy ladder and side-stroked silently to the other side of the moat. They crouched into the stunted, warm shadows and the ashes of the oak grove. Cybella paused in front of one blackened trunk.

"I will not forget, Simeon."

As she walked back across the valley with Grunius, Cybella thought of her unnamed stream in the wilderness west of Enclava in Archerland, its sweet flow now drowned in salt, and the tree in which she had abided as many rings counted the time within which she lived, unaware of its passage. That huge oak was now stunted, leafless and branchless, beneath the sea, turning to inhospitable stone. She hoarded the memory of the memory – for her experience itself had been a kind of memory at the time, a dream to be remembered when she woke up.

"And your thoughts?" Grunius asked.

"Of a time when I had no thoughts," she replied.

"I know. Are you sorry I brought you forth?"

"Oh no! Only sorry that nature involves such loss."

"It does involve conflict, true."

"But if you had not summoned me from that tree."

"You might have escaped anyway. Do not think of yourself at the bottom of the sea."

"I do not. But I do think of my tree at the bottom of the sea."

"Yes. But that, too, was nature's doing."

"And the fire? That was Mazlund's doing."

"That I cannot deny," Grunius said.

"Look what we found!"

A guard thrust Jerome into Mazlund's room of state.

"Ah, Jerome! It has been some time! What have you there?"

Jerome clung to a wicker basket in which he had the mushrooms he'd been gathering when one of Mazlund's patrols captured him. "Mushrooms."

"Ah, yes. As I recall Lisle enjoys them with her ribeyes."

How did Mazlund know that?

"Now, Jerome, since you are here, let me put a proposition before you."

"The same one as before?"

"Essentially. Yes. I need eyes and ears in their camp. You need report nothing that would compromise their security."

"Just local gossip?"

"You could say so, yes."

"But what would my value be to you if I delivered nothing of value?"

"I need to understand their life, its mosaic, its allegory. I hope, you see, to forge an alliance with your group. Knowing their ways will help me."

"Their weaknesses, you mean."

"Not necessarily. If I have some sense of who they are, I have a chance to appeal to them on that basis, to offer things to them that will bring some joy into their humdrum lives."

"You should know who they are by now!"

"You have a point, of course. But up to now it has been an adversarial relationship. You can help me toward a more conciliatory attitude."

"And I can be that handsome hussar?"

"As I promised before. And with the order of the Black Widow, Second Class on your tunic."

"Second Class?"

"Make that First Class. It would be one of two I have awarded."

"The other being to yourself?"

"True. The other advantage, Jerome, is that if we succeed in this diplomacy, you will become a person of some importance in the new dispensation."

"The hussar – would I be like you?"

"Like me?"

Jerome looked into Mazlund's eye. Deep beneath its calm surface, a fire burned.

"Like me? Why yes."

That would mean that Jerome would surrender his soul to become that lean, decorated member of the elite cavalry.

"You know the magic word, Jerome."

"Yes, I do... but I will not say it."

It was 'nularutan,' but Jerome did not utter the word.

"You prefer to remain a stunted dwarf, subject to the derision of all who lay eyes upon you? You can become a great... ah... personage in our emerging kingdom, a leader of..."

"Of other shapes that look like people, but serve a darker power."

"Oh, I'd hardly put it that way."

"There's no other way to put it, Mazlund."

Jerome was already a personage in his small community, and Lisle did not complain that he was not the dashing horseman of his own platonic dream of himself. Nor did he detect any scorn in her eyes. And, of course, once an agent of Mazlund's, Jerome would be required to provide more and more information about his group. He would ultimately be required to betray them some day not far off.

"And then, of course, you have to deal with that troublesome Troll."

How had Mazlund know about that! Did he need a spy at all? Yes, Tomaso had been a problem.

"He is merely a trifle anti-social."

Mazlund laughed.

Yes, thought Jerome. He found little joy in being a gnome, particularly since his role as guardian of the diamond mines of Archerland had long since been terminated. Now, he was just an unemployed freak. But he had enjoyed a certain perverse satisfaction in being different. Tomaso, with his gnarled face and huge, moonlike eyes, had attracted more attention from the few who encountered the group from Archerland. Jerome had felt like a creature even more marginalized than nature had made him to be.

Mazlund did not know that Tomaso and I have become friends, Jerome realized. He does need a spy! He thought he could use what he thinks he knows to divide us! Let him retain his ignorance.

"No," Jerome said.

"You are difficult to understand, Jerome. But then some people cannot be convinced of their own best interests. Perversity rules. However, should you change your mind, you know where to find me."

But perversity does not rule! Jerome thought. That is one thing I am learning.

Jerome reached up for his basket, which had been placed on a table.

Mazlund put his hand on the handle.

"And thank you for these excellent looking and obviously fresh mushrooms!"

Jerome scowled at Mazlund. Some perversity still exists! Jerome would return empty handed to the camp. But better that, thought Jerome as he left, than to go back without my soul.

"You are not cooperating with me!"

"Cooperating with you? Why should we?"

"Because I am the ruler here in TerraNova."

"We call it Otherland, Mazlund. And that you do not rule."

Mazlund had summoned Estrella after some of her people and members of his company had had a dispute about fishing in a nearby trout stream.

"Guard! To the prison with her!"

"I came under a flag of truce!"

"I renounce the truce. You are defying me! I gave you all those utensils!"

"I did not notice any conditions with the gift."

"A gift always carries conditions!"

"Perhaps. But a flag of truce conveys an obligation to the one who recognizes it."

"Anyone holding up a flag of truce takes her chances. Guard!"

"No wine this time?" she asked

But what else could she expect? Mazlund was a betrayer. Still she wondered, why the look of pain in his eye that she glimpsed just before she was led away? Gout perhaps.

Estrella was thirsty. She had been given a glass of water earlier, and had swallowed it too quickly. Now, she eyed the inch of liquid at the bottom of the glass. She held it up. It captured the gray light of her cell. She recalled the old song.

"I raise my glass to Archerland.
No enemies we fear,
For our land, we take our stand,
Let enemies beware."

And yet, as she watched the mysterious wind that wove the spider's webbing back and forth here in the deep, tomblike dungeon, she did feel fear. Her few friends were far away and she stood in a gray darkness behind oaken doors, below thick stones. And Archerland itself was a crumbled dream many fathoms beneath the sea.

She took that final sip of stale water.

Langar ran his tongue across his lip. My, that wine was good! It was one of the benefits of following Mazlund, a good cellar. But more than that, much more. He breathed in, and with that inward breath came the feeling of power. I am about to achieve power, he thought. As Mazlund's lieutenant, I will be one of the great men in this new kingdom of TerraNova. Mazlund does not trust von Beak or von Rodent and has only a minimal confidence in that sybarite, Vallarte. I am the one in whom he confides. I am the one whose plans he embraces. I have become indispensable to him.

He walked to the portal that looked south to the unnamed peninsula.

I will ask him to name it after me, he thought. And the others – the survivors of Archerland would have to bow to me! He had lived in the shadow of his brother, Mark. "Why can't you be more like Mark?" His parents did not say it in so many words, but he could overhear the thought. Mark the heir. Mark the favored son, given first choice at everything – from schools and ponies to ancestral swords and armor to wear on ceremonial occasions. Given the Cross of Archerland on his eighteenth birthday!

And Langar had looked on. People did not like him, he knew, compared to the smiling Mark, who would doff his bonnet to a wench selling cockles and mussels on the streets. But Langar could observe, and he could make people feel very uneasy about what he saw with those sharply-focused green eyes of his. He could read the deeds of others, sometimes before the others even discerned their own motivations.

The final battle had come on the beach below Corilus. Langar had seen his brother, the King, facing Linvallen, the traitor who had stolen Queen Glorimere. Langar could have intervened just before Linvallen had let his sword fall on Mark, but it was every man for himself at that point. And it had been too late only an instant later. Mark, of course, had delivered a fatal blow to Linvallen, so the two died as the tide came in that day, unaware of the great event that it was erasing. Langar had escaped the field. He was King at last! He had sought out Seraman, the unctuous politician, to help with the claim. He knew that his succession would be unpopular. But he was next in line! And who could challenge him? Estrella, of course. She would have the voice of the people.

But the earth had been uneasy by the time he got to the Castle of Peace. He and Seraman had scarcely had time to fashion a raft before the waters had rushed up from the shore, the waves turning brown with the rich soil of Archerland, pulling great trees up by the roots, flowing over the streams that only moments before had been rushing down to the ocean, cruising over the rooftops and pushing thatch into what seemed to be a rising flood but which was really the island sinking forever beneath the erasing sea.

And now the way to power was through Mazlund! Mark had been killed in a civil war he could have avoided. If he could see me now! Langar said to himself, smiling. And I will capture that prize that he could not hold – the splendid Glorimere!

He took another sip of wine. His future unfolded itself, as wide and fertile as the land that opened beneath his view. Was that just the wine? No – it was tomorrow speaking to him!

Umgalla stood on a promontory and gazed across the land. The sun, rising over the sea, was at his back, so that the world seemed to be creating itself, forming before his eyes, leaf by leaf, tree by tree and hillside by hillside in the unfolding light. The only stain along the spreading landscape was the Fortress, the grim, gray stones occupied by Mazlund and his Terror Troopers.

Why, Umgalla asked himself, must they be here? Is it, as the mythology of the visitors from Archerland had it, that once in a garden a man and a woman consumed a fruit forbidden to them by their God? That may have summoned evil to the world, but it was also, as Umgalla saw it, a necessary step. How can we know what is good unless an opposite exists? And into the goodness of this land – its forests and their game, its steams, punctuated by the leap of trout and salmon, its fields asway with maize and wheat, its vast reach going to valleys and mountains as yet seen only by the eyes of wild animals, not yet contemplated by the mind of a human being – had come this evil.

And it was not just that Mazlund was bad, the epitome of badness. It was his ideas. Empire. What did that mean? It meant that those who were not servants of the goal of absolute power over all things visible and invisible (like thought) were enemies. It meant that ideology was imposed upon geography. The land became subservient to a concept. Mazlundianism. But the land resisted. It was nature. And the people who inhabited the land also resisted. Mazlund's "Ownership Society," as he called it, meant that he owned the people. Not yet, Umgalla thought. Long ago, the Conquistadors, as they called themselves, had tried to enslave Umgalla's people. It had been a terrible time, a time of executions for no cause, a time of injustice visited upon a people who had a strong sense of what was just, even if they had no written laws. But the people had survived. The conquerors had left without holds full of gold. And many of their galleons had been sunk by a storm that leapt up just as their weighed their anchors. It had been, the legends suggested, an act of the gods of the natural world against those who had tried to turn nature to their own narrower purposes.

The people from Archerland had understood. And now they were here. And they, too, though small in numbers and weak in arms, would resist the power of Mazlund.

Umgalla raised his arms to the scene now spread before him as the sun threw his shadow across the land.

"Come what may," he said aloud. "You will survive. And we will survive within this larger purpose that we cannot name but that we can see each time the sun brings it to light again."

Estrella brushed at the moss that covered the stone. Why? she wondered. But yes messages had been inscribed here – with what? – the buckles of belts? The handles of broken swords? The nails from rotten shoes?

"You who read this are not the first
Imprisoned thus. You are not alone,
Believe that as you read this stone,
And with hope renewed, slake your thirst."

Yes, she thought. Knowing that others have suffered is helpful. But I also thirst for water as well as for spirit. And as she thought this, Estrella heard a sound, as if some soft fabric were being torn. No! It was the sound of water. The sound of a spring percolating from some deep-down freshlet! Where?

Yes – at the moss-shrouded corner of the cell. Again, her fingers were busy. The moss was damp. Then water flowed across her fingers and into her cupped hands.

So small – a sip of water. So taken for granted. But here it was as if she drank in hope again. She would escape. That was the truth. The details merely needed to be worked out. And God was in the details, as she had learned so often, but had almost forgotten. What is it about the damp light of a dungeon that squeezes their identity from people? Tyrants know. But she thought of the Apostle in prison who sang and got others to sing with him and startled the drowsy jailers above. A song rose within her as her eyes roved the mossy stones for a way out. But even if she did not find a way out, she knew that the fear that had lain beneath her hopelessness had melted away.

> "I sing again to Archerland,
> with voice of hope anew,
> For Archerland I raise my hand,
> And to that land am true."

And she realized that the covenant she had framed with her people had been ratified. Contact with the power that makes all compacts meaningful had been established at last. But of what benefit was that good news when she was languishing here in this dungeon? What good are isolated insights? She was, after all, in TerraNova, as Mazlund had named it.

Langar held the key in his right hand.

"This is the key, little man, but it will do you no good."

The key was suspended from ring that ran inside a wooden handle.

"Now you can watch it float out of sight. And with it, your hopes of seeing her alive again."

He flung the handle into the river, the key spinning over and over again through the fading light until it landed in the swift flow of the stream.

But, from out of no where, came Sheba.

"No, Sheba," George called from behind the dog. "The river is too rapid!"

But the dog took off from the shore, all four paws extended, and was soon headed downstream, partly swimming, partly pulled by the flow of the river toward the waterfall.

George took Langar by the collar of his shirt and raised him up roughly.

"You, Langar, will pay for this!"

"He has locked Estrella in the dungeon," Jerome said. "That was the key to her cell!"

As George turned toward Jerome's words, Langar hit George with a backhand swipe and ran toward the Fortress.

"Poor Sheba!" George said, wiping blood from his mouth. "How did you know about the key?"

"I slipped into the Fortress as they were changing the guard. I hung on the side of one of their horses after the cavalry dismounted. They keep the keys in the keep, of course, and I took this one, hoping to sneak down and let her free. But Langar saw me and chased me. I do not run as fast as he does."

"They have to use the key to open the cell to feed her! Without the key..."

He let his conclusion find its place on Jerome's crestfallen face.

"I have done more harm than good," Jerome said.

But as they wandered disconsolately back toward their settlement, they heard a scratching on the leaves behind them.

"Sheba!"

And Sheba held the wooden handle in her jaws.

She dropped the key at George's feet. Both George and Jerome laughed as Sheba shook herself, sending a chatoyant rainbow across the pathway.

IX.

The light from the single opening high on the stone wall moved up the further wall and died. Only a spitting sconce down the corridor sent any light into her cell. It made shadows of the bars of her door against the wall above her cot. She would be reminded of her imprisonment even as she slept. The spurt of hope she had felt when interrogated by Mazlund began to fade. Her joy as she drank at the spring began to dry up. I must not, Estrella thought, surrender to despair. That is the last refuge for people who have given up. And they enjoy it! Not for me, she insisted. This is a process – and it is not always steady!

She thought of the mother and her sons, executed one by one by the evil king, Antiochus. This was after the temple came to celebrate Bacchus and had become the home of Jupiter Olympius. I, she thought, could never be as steadfast as she. She shook her head, aware of this flow of self-doubt. It was also a loss of faith, she knew, belief retreating like a tide to whatever ocean held it in reserve. Or – did it just dry up like water pulled from the sea by the summer sun? If so, how did one get it back again?

And, though she wondered how her sons were and though she missed them with an intensity that at times seemed to overwhelm her, she held on. She noticed how hard it was to think without another person near to whom to talk. But if I talk to myself, she thought, I will go another way to madness. I have found the small spring within me. I must keep it alive!

She thought of her own life, coming from a humble farm in Tidal Plain, home territory of King Paul the First, who had started out with only hopeful prophecies, a large white dog, Major, and a promise that he would learn more during his journey to retake the land from the Darkforce. How much he had done! She had done little, but, she reminded herself, she had done what she could. She had mastered the art of stone-slinging: the selection of suitable stones, the fitting them into the pouch of the sling, the warmup twist of the sling above the head to measure weight against distance, the aiming, sling held in the direction of the toss, and then whip of the sling and the crucial flip of the wrist to send the stone toward its target. And when that target was hit – the satisfying flow of intention back to the following-through arm of the slinger.

She described a circle above her head.

And she had learned to teach the technique to others, so that she was soon Commander of Archerland's Stone-Slinger Brigade. They had surprised one of Mazlund's regiments one day, just as it was about to outflank Archerland's tiny army, and had driven the enemy away in disarray, its commanders believing that it was the victim of some sort of rock slide that threatened to bury them. Estrella had discovered that the things of nature – in this case the stones indigenous to Archerland – could defeat the Darkforce. The Darkforce had the power of illusion and trickery and ruses de guerre and had even once impressed the bodies of the dead into their ranks in the smelliest battle she had ever fought, but nature was superior to all of that. Young Paul had learned that on his journey. And Estrella had also learned that as she applied her skills in combat against Mazlund and his Terror Troopers.

Yes, she thought, but how does that help me now?

She looked around her cell, trembling in the truckle of the distant torch. The far side was almost covered with moss. Was that the north side? It would be were it a tree. Moss does not like light. Moss likes moisture. If so...

She went to that side of her cell – it took only a step – and began to pull the moss from the walls. As she did so, she could hear the sound of water. Yes! It was the river that ran around the Fortress and formed the moat. She was on the north side of the Fortress. How does that help me? she asked. If I escape, I will know where I am. But these stones!

She heard the grating of an iron door opening and waited while the lantern of a guard made jagged shadows along the corridor outside that angled through the bars on the door of her cell. She had moved to the south side.

"I am still here," she said.

"Why am I not surprised?" said the guard.

The lantern pulled its shadows back along the footsteps of the guard to the iron door.

The light was dead in the barred window high above Estrella's head, but she continued pulling the moss away from the stone. And then, it was not stone, but wood. And the moss came quickly. The wood itself was rotten and pulled free in her hands like an old sponge. Soon, she was looking down at the river, flowing blackly past the green stones below. How far below? How deep is it here? How cold is the water?

She could not hesitate, however. And, the next time the guard came past her cell on his hourly rounds, he was surprised.

In many ways, Mazlund preferred the human shape. He could smile from above his decorations – the intricate Order of the Spider, First Class, below his throat, the ornate Order of the Rat, First Class, the bleak, but impressive Iron Crow, and the many campaign medals he had issued himself on the left side of his silken tunic. He enjoyed the clink of silver and gold as he moved through his challenging daily schedule. Of course, he thought, had I only won any of those campaigns their memorialization would mean more to me! He knew that his eye-patch, black velvet surrounded by tiny pearls, was intimidating, but that it lent him an aura of mystery. And he had enjoyed the wines of Archerland – the smooth, dry assertion of their own superiority. The best of them even smirked, but discretely. The wines warmed him, made him feel almost human. But while they could moderate the sizzle of rage that lived at his core, they could not drown it. And, at times, when he had unwisely had one glass too many, he found himself striding around on uneven steps, uttering imprecations for no reason, and terrifying the servants who scuttled in and out on various missions.

Mazlund was in such a mood now, partly because the pinot noir that accompanied his roast mocked him with its assumptions of a status it did not deserve. Did he find a self-image in the wine? He dared not ask.

He was in malfettle because he had considered his plan. He knew it to be a good plan. He knew it to be a plan that could bring about the reconciliation between his party of the Fortress and the ragged band of survivors across the several valleys. Reconciliation? Yes! He dismissed the real word, which was subordination. Subjugation? No!

He covered his intentions, even in his own mind, with a glaze of rationalization. Wonderful invention, these human words! What rankled him then?

At least I am not giving her to him! To Langar! No. Mazlund laughed bitterly. He gets Glorimere. But I... A breath of humanity, of wish, desire, of a word he could not utter, entered him. He felt for a moment that he was suffocating!

"Chirac! Wine!"

"Yes, Archfiend of Fearsome Activity? Will you select from the..."

"Any bottle will do! Just bring it!"

Chirac was offended. He had been about to provide a choice between a medium bodied red whose complexity was almost insolent and a pinot grigio that was at once soft and almost aggressively dry. But not now! He took great pride in his suzerainty. Mazlund's cellar was Chirac's kingdom and he did not savor insults to his mastery of the grape. A failure to select from the almost infinite variety of vintages was a reproof he could scarcely tolerate.

He bit back a response and slumped off without a word.

Even the servants! All things move against my will, which should be supreme! Mazlund muttered to himself.

A guard entered.

"Sire of All that is Sinister..."

"Yes, yes."

"She has escaped!"

His first thought was, I know that, idiot! But his second thought was, that is not what this idiot means.

Chirac entered holding a bottle out for Mazlund's inspection.

"Get out of here, you fool!" Mazlund shouted.

Chirac turned without bowing. How had Mazlund known that this was an ancient Burgundy on the edge of vinegary disaster? That one eye of his must be very sharp!

"But George went to get her!" Jerome said.

"George?" Grunius asked.

"Yes. He had the key to her cell!"

"But the word I pick up from the alarms and excursions along the roadway is that she has escaped!"

"Now George is in that Fortress."

"Looking for Estrella," Grunius said.

"I'm afraid so," Jerome said.

"We gain nothing, then. We merely exchange one prisoner for another."

Estrella crouched in a copse, listening to the clink of a mounted patrol on the roadway. She shivered, her clothes still damp from her chilly swim, and the cool shadows of evening closing in. But good for the shadows! she thought. They'd find me otherwise.

"She cannot have gone far," said Mazlund's captain. "Let's go down to the eastern bend in the road. She'd be trying to go in that direction."

And, of course, she was. But she noticed something. The troop as it continued on did not seem as numerous as it had when it had paused near her hiding place. Was that merely the difference between the sound as it came toward her and the sound as it left her? She knew that sounds differed – even the same sound, like the silence before birdsong in the morning, and the silence after. Of course, the latter silence was suffused with rising light. The former had been accompanied only by final stars.

She dared a crawl through the ancient leaves and looked out at the road.

Yes! The moon threw the shadows of two horses into the trees on the other side. Mazlund's captain had hoped to trap her by taking his main force away. Well, that would not work, but she was very cold. She would almost give up were that to bring her close to a camp fire or hearth again. She shivered again, a reaction resulting partly from her thought of the chill night coming on as she crouched within a hoofbeat or two of the enemy.

George took his place beside the guard.

"You are new?"

"Yes, sir."

"Well, join me then. We are going to try to get some food into the cell for the Princess Estrella. Some fool stole the key."

"I will hold the tray for you, while you open this gate."

The guard did so. They moved through the gate.

"I will take it to her," George said. "Vallarte has ordered you to report to him."

"Vallarte? What does he want with me?"

"Ask him."

"I don't..."

"It will not do to keep him waiting."

The guard turned and marched briskly up the corridor.

George put the tray down, put the key in the lock, turned it, and opened the door to an empty cell.

One of the horses gave an impatient snort.

"Well," said a soldier. "If she is hiding nearby, she certainly heard your horse!"

"I could not help that," said the other soldier. "But I agree. She's not anywhere near where we are. And, it's getting cold. Let's report back. They are having a Full Moon Madness Party at the barracks tonight."

"Yes. Mazlund will let us uncork some of the good wine. Let's wait one more minute, then go!"

And Estrella knew that she would soon be across the road. She would pick up the highway to the east as soon as she thought it was safe to do so. Meanwhile, the moon rising to its majesty and pulling all waters toward her magnificence would guide Estrella through these northern woods.

And then, without warning, she sneezed.

Immediately, George saw the tattered door – more like fabric than wood — through which his mother had escaped! Good! He pulled the tray into the cell and left it in plain sight – that would add to their bafflement – and even took a couple of munches from a muffin. His adventure had made him hungry. He heard the outer door begin to scrape open. An angry guard returning to upbraid him. He swallowed half of the muffin – blueberries! yes, they were in season – and ducked through the outer door. He was on a walkway above the moat. He paused for a moment, dove, and swam under water with the current until he had to breathe. He heard shouts behind him, but not "There he is!" – just the general shouts of an alarm and the confused scurryings hither and yon that accompany a perceived emergency . Something was poking him in the stomach. Yes – it was the handle of the key that he had brought with him on this wild gander chase! He should have known that his mother would find a way to escape! Still, it had been something to remember, and he would keep the key as a souvenir of his passage in and out of Mazlund's castle. No, a memento. He had not yet learned to spell souvenir. He climbed from the moat where it became the single branch of the river again and ran into the eastward-slanting shadows of the trees. He was cold, but, more than that, he was hungry! He regretted leaving all that food behind, but then he had been in a hurry.

"She is not back?" George asked, huddled into a blanket.

"We have not seen her," Harry said.

"But she escaped before I did! She should have been back hours ago!"

George thought for a moment.

"Still, the roads are full of Mazlund's patrols tonight."

"You are sure she escaped?" Harry asked.

"Oh yes. An old door in the wall. She had made a hole in it just large enough for her. I had to duck to get through. Wait a minute!"

"What?" Harry asked.

"I know where she is!"

"You do?"

"Where she must be," George said less positively. "Gregg! Let's get your boat out!"

Estrella ran more deeply into the woods. The two horsemen had to dismount.

"Let's follow her!"

"Shouldn't we report to Langar?"

"No! We'll lose her. Come on!"

Estrella heard the men, hardly experienced woodsmen, crashing through the underbrush behind her, and cursing as a twig lashed across their faces. But she was being forced on to a peninsula that narrowed toward the sea on one side and a cove on the other. She knew that a guard post stood on the seaward side of the sliver of land, so she headed toward the cove. Still, what good would that do her? It would merely delay her recapture. And this time she would be held in chains!

Gregg and George swung around the cape.

"Coming about!" Gregg called. George ducked.

"That guard post will see us!" George said.

"We can't help that! The moon is right behind us!"

They heard a bugle sound from the shore. Assembly! The shadows of soldiers lining up played against silver trees.

Estrella edged along the peninsula wondering whether she should simply swim away from her pursuit. The two men following her had dropped back, but now soldiers from the guard post, only a half-mile away, were coming down the road toward her. The water will be cold!

The boat slipped into the cove.

"Not too close!" George shouted.

"I know. We don't want to get within spear-range of those soldiers."

"I hope she sees us."

The soldiers had stopped on the shore and were pointing in the direction of the boat.

"The soldiers do," Gregg said.

"How will we reach her?"

Gregg shook his head. Estrella would see them, but if she made a move in their direction, or if they attempted to bring the boat into shallow water... It was hopeless.

X.

"Wait," Mazlund said. "You say the tray was inside the cell?"

"Yes, Regent of Rage. The door was locked. The tray was on a table. Only a muffin had suffered a bite or two. We had planned to hand the food, bit by bit, to Queen Estrella, to continue to feed her as you had commanded, so that your reputation for hospitality would not suffer."

Mazlund began an angry reply, but it was blocked by his bafflement.

"And the ancient door on the further wall had been shredded?"

"As far as we could tell, Highness of Horrors. The door to the cell remains locked."

"But that cannot be! The key was stolen. Langar threw it into the river and watched it disappear! This young guard who joined you cannot have gone through that door as if it were a morning mist!"

"No, Dread Decider of Doom. But the young man – if human he be – is no longer within the Fortress."

"Are you sure?"

"We have searched, Prince of Panic."

"But, by your account, he entered the cell, took a bite of muffin, then fled."

"It may have been the Queen who took a bite of muffin, Sinister Sire. And it was more than a bite."

"Who consumed the fragment of muffin is beside the point! Your version of events is not plausible."

The guard, having run out of Mazlundian honorifics, shrugged.

"Search again! And bring this impostor to me when he is found."

The guard thumped his chest and backed away from Mazlund toward the throneroom's portal.

Mazlund slumped on his throne. It was not that bad news had come to him. He had received bad news all during his long combat with the forces and people of Archerland. But this? It was like one of those locked-room mysteries he sometimes read when he was bored. The solution usually was that something or someone had been in that locked room before it was locked. But the guard was to be believed at least as far as his statement that the tray had been outside the cell and then had somehow gotten inside. That strange little detail about the bite or two out of the blueberry muffin – it had been blueberry, had it not? – supported the contention that the tray had somehow filtered through the locked door. But how? Mazlund felt the kind of tremor that came from something unknown. It was not just the confusion, however, which poisoned the attitude of one so absolute. He was being asked to accept the possibility that a larger power than he could contradict was at work. No! he said, loud enough for the word to echo within his head. Never!

"Look!" George shouted.

And there, in the water along a ribbon of moonlight reaching toward the mainland, was a head below a waving arm.

Gregg pulled the tiller to his chest.

"I am going past her, then come about. Be ready to haul her aboard. And don't get pulled in yourself!"

In a moment or two more, Estrella, dripping and shivering was aboard, as Gregg headed to sea again.

"Get below," Gregg said. "Blankets and a small barrel of rum!"

"And it stinks of old bait!" George warned.

"That I can stand," Estrella said, laughing. "I smell just a bit like a wet dog myself. But warmth and a tot! And my nose is pretty well stuffed up anyway!"

"No!" Neutralon said. "You, Estrella are needed here. You claim that no hierarchy pertains to this group of survivors, but a natural order has developed. You are the leader here."

He looked at the group assembled around the fire. The light flickered on their faces, but it did not show a single doubt in any eye.

"I, on the other hand, a late arrival who found you already well-established, even thriving, am expendable."

"No one of us is to be considered that way!" Estrella said.

"That is a noble sentiment, dear Estrella, but you know that others have had to sacrifice themselves in the larger cause. And, let me hasten to add, that I intend to return to this very fire and to your much-prized company as soon as I can do so."

"I am still convinced that I should go," Estrella said. "I have been there before."

"Experience is no doubt a great instructor," Neutralon replied, "but you neglect one crucial qualification that I possess."

"And what is that?" Grunius asked.

"With the possible exception of you, Grunius, once Mazlund's Master of Special Projects, and possibly Jerome, were he to volunteer to become a spy, I am the only one here who can gain admission to the Fortress."

"Yes, that is probably true," Estrella conceded.

"But why?" asked Harry. "I could sneak in and find that door."

Neutralon smiled at the young man.

"My position in Enclava dictated a necessary neutrality. Oh, I was always loyal to Archerland, but I had to play a game. And while Mazlund may not trust me – he trusts no one, of course – he will not mistrust me. One of the problems of his position is that evil is partial and that any effort to make it total involves compromise. I think that he will accept me as a valuable ally."

"I think you are right," Cybella said. "He is forever seeking treaties and alliances with us."

"Not so much to bolster his own power," Estrella said, "but to undermine ours. Any compromise with true evil really is surrender."

"True," Neutralon said. "And so you see..."

"Yes," Estrella said. "It is you who must go."

Mazlund felt something cross his eye. Something between him and the sun!

Yes! Just diving to attack was one of the eagles of Umgalla's Raptor Squadron!

Mazlund had been out on solo patrol, one of the few moments he could enjoy away from the heavy weight of rule. He no longer flew formation. His depth perception did not permit him to navigate as flight leader. Nor could he make the minute corrections demanded when he was on the wing of another crow. So he flew solo. He had told himself not to indulge himself this way, that he endangered the greater bad in such indulgence, but he also knew that he alone could gather the intelligence needed for his strategies. There are old pilots and bold pilots, he mused, but there are no old, bold pilots. But now it was time for tactics.

Mazlund knew from long experience that he must assess his position, that of his enemy, and their relative strengths and weaknesses in an instant. He did so, already into a steep turn as he considered what his opponent would be doing. His enemy would have to alter the angle of his dive out of the sun. Mazlund climbed briefly, then rolled away from his opponent in a dive. The other must change direction again. Mazlund climbed again and banked into a steep turn to the right. Yes! Now he had this eagle turning with him! He was lighter and more maneuverable and so could out turn the other bird. That would give him a chance to call for help.

He did so. "Squee, Crowl, Squee! Squee, Crowl, Squee!"

And, from a nearby rookery, he saw black wings rising.

But his opponent had reversed his own turn and was now sliding in on Mazlund's tail. The talons were closer!

Mazlund tipped his wings back abruptly, braking his flight with a shudder. The eagle overflew him, those great grips just grazing Mazlund's top cockpit feathers. Close!

Mazlund glided in the opposite direction, as a three-ship formation of his Crow Command flew past. He looked up from the safety of a blue spruce and his birds encountered the eagle. Black feathers flew. It was an uneven contest. The crows clattered. The eagle was silent. Shortly, three black birds spiraled slowly to the ground, dead wings riding out to create a moment of lift against the game that gravity was playing with them. A few feathers followed, their white tips inscribing random circles as they fell.

Good pilots all, Mazlund thought with some regret. Still, that's what I pay them for! He was not as good as he had been. His single eye did not give him the kind of depth perception he had once enjoyed, and his accommodation – his ability to swing without blinking from an object very close to something far away – had deserted him. He had almost banged his beak into the trunk of the tree while landing just now and he still recalled his embarrassing collision with a flying squirrel only months before. The squirrel, having recovered from a nasty spin, had admonished him rudely upon landing. A squirrel!

The eagle towered above Mazlund's perch and searched with keenly focused eyes. Mazlund ducked beneath a branch that made his blue-black feathers invisible. The eagle pulled up into the green twilight, turning gold as he ascended, did an Immelmann turn at the top of his loop, and winged away.

Showoff! Mazlund muttered.

Seraman had seen enough. He had little or no belief himself, having served too many masters, but he knew that he could no longer serve Mazlund. That, he thought, is partly because of Mazlund, partly because of Langar, who has risen to such a station, and partly something I cannot put my finger on.

He tapped the left side of his chest and felt a returning signal from under the silk.

Yes, he thought, it has something to do with a feeling. That in serving Mazlund I do wrong? He laughed at himself, but his cynical chuckle gave way to a nodding of his own head. Yes. He had been a double agent for so long that he did not know what identity to believe, yet some strange face stared at him from an inner mirror. That's it. My own sense of right and wrong will not leave me. Or, perhaps it has developed because of my proximity to Mazlund. One does not necessarily surrender to that malign presence. And, negative role models are usually more powerful than good ones. At least one can say, I don't have to be like that! I will try to slip away from here – I have had plenty of practice in sliding around! – and get into the camp of the Archerland survivors. I must warn them. If Mazlund cannot get his way with those people, he intends to attack.

"You seem preoccupied, Seraman?"

Seraman spun his head in Langar's direction.

"Me?"

"Obviously. I startled you."

"Oh no, I was just thinking."

"You think too much."

"You claim that I think too much?"

"Yes. I scheme. I make plans. I conspire. You? You think."

"True."

"And tomorrow..."

"Yes. But it is always tomorrow, isn't it."

"That's exactly what I mean! But come, Mazlund wishes us to go over his final order of battle."

"Go along. I'll come presently."

"You will come now, Seraman. I want to keep an eye on you."

How, Seraman wondered, would he get away? It had to be soon. But Langar was suspicious.

Estrella carried herself with confidence after her escape, but her thoughts returned occasionally to the dark bars that shone across the wall of her cell. Could she thank God for her deliverance? She was still not sure of her place in any design. And that doubt meant that her belief was itself shaky. Was it all mere chance that had delivered her from the fall of Archerland into the sea and from the prison of Mazlund here in this new land? Doubts, doubts, doubts! I am pulled back and forth, she thought.

> "What should we do, here
> in this wild place?
> Is that your hand there
> in the leaf, your face
> in the still pool beside
> the bank. You hide
> again in the sunrise
> and with stars open eyes
> upon us? Or is the night
> just a loss of light?
> Do you have a voice?
> Do we have a choice?"

She could not pray, only ask questions. Then she heard a familiar voice – Kermath!

> Yes, you always have a choice.
> Show us what it is!
> You already know.
> Do I?

But that had been Kermath's voice. And so I must learn what I already know.

"And what brings you to these shores?"

"Wind and tide."

"I assumed so. I meant what motive brings you come to my Fortress?"

"Clearly the promise of sunlit days, moonlit nights by sleepy lagoons, steaming plates of delicacies, your superb cellar..."

"Yes, the wine is good, but spare me the irony, Neutralon."

"You know me, Mazlund. I have survived by placing my lot with winners. I saw the camp of the Archerland remnants. Pathetic. You could waft them away with a sweep of your left hand."

"Yes, but I am trying for something else this time."

"Not just total power?"

"Legitimacy. I have been missing the point all these centuries. If I am the rightful ruler, even the power-that-I-cannot-name must recognize me."

"You have a point, of course. And I..."

"Yes. You were a Prince of Archerland. But how do I know that I can trust you?"

"You don't, of course. Do you trust Seraman?"

"No."

"But he serves you."

"Yes."

"Langar?"

"Not on your life!"

"But he serves you."

"Seraman and Langar serve themselves. I have incorporated their energies into my purposes."

"And I, once a Prince of Archerland..."

"Yes. You, too, serve yourself, but..."

"I can also serve a purpose."

Umgalla was about to leave the encampment after a visit with Estrella.

He looked carefully at Glorimere, who had accompanied him to the end of the woods. He saw – though it was invisible – the blue wisp that surrounded her. It was a sign of lost hope. And she was so young! But then, he realized, she had been born to royalty and had never had a chance to grow up and make her own choices, and mistakes. Because her choices had been made for her, mistakes would follow. And something else in that wreath of numinous blue – a father's regret. That was the human element. Umgalla understood it. You knew that your sons would play their dangerous games, scrape their knees, bloody their noses. But for a daughter? The father could only fear. And Glorimere's father had feared for her and had been disappointed in her. And she knew it. Umgalla thought of his own daughter, Majorum. He was helpless, as was any father who had a daughter. But he did not fear for her. Or, if he did, he knew that she would never be surrounded by the aura of her father's disappointment. And he had begun to realize that Majorum would never give off the scent of loneliness, as did Glorimere.

"You are young, yet, Glorimere," he said to her.

She looked at him with an unguarded expression, as if to say, how did you know what I was thinking?

"Perhaps," she said, "but there are times…"

"When the world is on your shoulders?"

"That, yes, but when you feel that you can do nothing about it. That you had your chance."

He put a fatherly hand on each of her shoulders and smiled at her.

"I know little about what you call history. But I believe that the willingness to serve usually finds a purpose."

She seemed to sense the strength flowing from his fingers.

"Do you believe that?" she asked.

"Yes."

She smiled. It was the first smile coming from something deeper than her facial muscles that the old man had seen.

Seraman looked into Langar's eyes.

If I can, Seraman thought, I will.

And he cast the depth of his glance directly into the dark center of those eyes.

Yes! He had induced fear.

"Merely the inevitable moment of nervousness before the combat is joined," Langar mumbled to himself, responding to the strange inner tremble that almost escaped to his index finger as it pointed at Mazlund's map.

"Of course," Seraman said. "You seem certain that Mazlund will attack."

"Yes, he is losing patience with this diplomacy."

"Yes. Diplomacy does require patience. Have another glass of this excellent Chardonnay."

"Yes, yes, I will," Langar said, eagerly holding his glass toward the bottle that Seraman twisted expertly into the glass.

And another after that, Seraman thought, watching the pupils of Langar's eyes widen and lose their focus.

I will soon be on my way! Seraman thought.

"I am going to scout along their flanks," he said to Mazlund. "To make sure they have no pickets out tonight."

"Good!" said Mazlund. "Report back to me when you have done so. Langar,.you go to bed. You will be no good to me if and when I need you unless you do."

"But..."

Mazlund glared at Langar.

"Off with you! Now!"

Langar staggered off. Seraman bowed his way out and went to the stables to saddle his horse.

"No!" Neutralon said.

"No?"

"We categorically refuse your offer," Neutralon said.

"We?"

"Those who have survived the disappearance of Archerland."

"Oh, I thought that you were employing the royal plural, as befits a Prince of Enclava."

"No royalty exists in this new world."

"Oh? I am ruler of TerraNova."

"TerraNova?"

"It is the name I have given this place otherwise unknown to cartography. And I – I should say 'we,' since I speak in my role as royal being – have the power to name."

"Naming does not necessarily mean anything!"

"It means everything. It means that I – we – define the world."

"You merely label it."

"But on to the point. My wish – our wish – is to ally with Queen Glorimere. No more, no less. A simple request, even a humble one. And yet you oppose that."

"We of what was Archerland do oppose your wish."

"But why? An alliance would benefit both groups. Your people need the protection that my superior military can provide."

"Oh yes, Mazlund. Your superior military – and I grant that you have one – would make us prisoner. This alliance would merely add to your subjects. It would bring no benefits to us."

"Better living conditions! Better food! Freedom from fear of..."

"Of the native population? No! We have made friends with them."

"But they could turn on you at any moment."

"Why would they? We are developing the mutually beneficial relationship that you describe. Or do you mean freedom of fear from you? To place ourselves in your hands, as you propose, would make our worst fears come true. All that would accomplish would be for us to submit to your narrative. We would lose our own."

"Do you not miss your life in Enclava?"

"I miss the place. The view from my upper room. My tapestry."

"Ah yes – that tapestry! Do you not miss your position as a ruler? I could give you that back again, make you my deputy. You would be able to see the cape to the south across the woodland from your chamber. And you could make decisions in favor of your people, as you call them. They would be better off by far with a friend in power."

Neutralon paused.

"In return for?"

"Your persuasive voice in favor of the alliance I propose."

What harm could it do? Mazlund was likely to wipe them out anyway with one sweep of his Saber-brigade. Neutralon could see the preparations – the armorers at work, the cavalry drills, the sharpening of swords. This way, Neutralon could mitigate Mazlund's malignity and rage. If he could get a written agreement!

"And so, shall we come to terms?" Mazlund asked.

Neutralon felt himself falling into the old habits – negotiation, seeking elements that favored each party, trade-offs. He had lived that way for all of his life.

Mazlund pulled a rolled-up parchment from his silken sleeve.

"Peruse this document."

Neutralon held it in both hands and scanned the elegant writing with his eyes.

"Seems straightforward enough. Wait a minute. 'In blood'?"

"That merely seals the agreement. It signals commitment."

"I should say so! Wait – what is this business about 'the soul of the undersigned is hereby granted to the authority that has drawn up this contract'?"

"Standard clause."

"That's you?"

"I represent that authority, yes."

Neutralon pretended to re-read the scroll. He had equivocated in the past, saying one thing, meaning another, concealing what his tapestry told him when one of Mazlund's commanders would visit him. And he had been scorned by both parties. Since the first day of his encounter with the band of survivors in this new land, he had been accepted. Indeed, he had been entrusted with this embassy to this enemy, whom his followers called The Duke of Darkness. He realized that, for once, he had a way of affecting the story!

"So I would betray myself as well as my people."

"Hardly! You win for yourself the most coveted of positions, an office from which you bestow benefits upon your people."

"And in blood!"

"Merely a formality."

"On behalf of what is left of Archerland, I will have to think about it."

Mazlund laughed.

"On behalf of yourself," he said.

"Well, yes. I grant that much."

He had to gain time. But not much time existed. To prepare for war, Neutralon knew, was tantamount to going to war. It is almost impossible to reverse a mobilization. That door to that other world was below the place where he stood. He must find a way to get to it soon!

"You had best choose as I wish, Neutralon. Whatever you decide, I will prevail."

"That is for a power larger than you possess to decide, for all of your vaunted cavalry, Mazlund."

"We will see."

"Yes, we will."

How much time did he have? Neutalon wondered. A day. Two days? Mazlund was impatient.

"I will consider your proposal, Mazlund, but will return to my people without signing the document. I am neutral, but inclining your way."

"Some rationalization!" Mazlund said. "That is merely indecision!"

"Much of what we do is rationalized. I prefer to think of it as sublimation."

"You bandy words."

"No, Mazlund," Neutralon said. "You are the bandier of language. You must always rationalize. You have lost the single most important element of your being. Sublimation is an acceptance of one's own limits. The process sometimes allows for an improvement in whatever situation cannot be immediately resolved. If not, one recognizes the impossibility of a resolution. You can never improve your situation."

"You have twenty-four hours," Mazlund said.

XI.

"Who goes?"

"A friend."

"Dismount. Approach slowly."

Seraman moved toward the sentry, who held a torch up.

"Seraman!"

"Yes. Prince Harry?"

"Harry. We have no princes here. What do you want with us?"

"I bring news."

"You have been of the enemy's camp, Seraman. You probably bring false tidings meant to entrap us in some way."

"I understand your caution, Harry. But let me speak to Estrella."

"All right. Tie your horse there. Then follow me."

Harry looked up the pathway to where it met the sky. The leaves, green as grapes, glittered like a fountain above him. What was it – the way the light played on them? The way shadows turned to brightness as the pathway climbed into the trees? Yes, but it was the reach of that last tree into the sky! Somehow that felt like the future to him. He ran up the path. He had been relieved as guard at last and was on his way to meet Majorum.

"He has refined his plan. He wants only Glorimere," Seraman said.

"Me?"

"Yes, he will marry you to Langar."

"No!"

"That is his plan. Mazlund is negotiating the agreement with Neutralon even as I speak. Mazlund believes that the marriage will confer legitimacy on his own rule, a kind of earthly validation through the royal throne of Archerland for his own demonic dispensation."

"How do we know we can trust you?" Estrella asked.

"What would be my motive in lying about this?" Seraman asked.

"Obviously, to create in us a false sense of security."

"That would work only if you were prepared to surrender Glorimere."

"Which, of course, we will not do," Estrella said.

Seraman nodded.

"That means that we must fight him," George said.

"I think you are right," Seraman said. "And that means that if I had a devious motive here it would be to tempt your forces to battle. As it is, I am warning you so that you can prepare. Mazlund is mobilizing. Either that..."

"Or I marry Langar," Glorimere said.

"And that is not an option," Estrella said.

"He believes that this marriage would solidify his own rule?" Jerome asked.

"Even in a wilderness, such vainglory finds its place," Estrella said.

"I, too, am incredulous," Tomaso said.

"It would also weaken us," Estrella said.

"Yes," said Seraman. "It would eliminate your resistance to Mazlund."

"Yes," said Lisle, "simply by linking us. We would be in his power."

"And that we cannot permit," Estrella said. "The issue is larger than Glorimere."

Perhaps it is, Glorimere thought, but if these few attempt to defeat Mazlund in battle, these few will perish.

Mazlund smiled as Seraman and Langar left him. Mazlund had let it be known that he wished that Gorimere marry Langar. If that did work out, fine! he thought. His own army was almost ready. He could sense Seraman's growing doubts about his allegiance to the Darkforce. If Seraman were to warn that ragtag bunch from Archerland, they would have no choice but to meet him on the field. Still, Mazlund wished he had a further plan. Just in case. He had been overconfident in the past. But not this time! No matter which way things developed, Mazlund thought, they will go my way. He turned the bottle up on top of his glass, but it was almost empty. The best he could muster was a mocking trickle.

"Blast!"

H. R. Coursen

But then he laughed. A minor setback within the grand scheme of things. And he controlled that design.

"Chirac! More wine!" he shouted. "Something fresh and crisp, with a fruity flavor, and no insolent backtalk!"

He rubbed his hands together. He could feel the future even as the stars wheeled their zodiac in that direction. Would that the time would pass more quickly!

"Monarch of Malice, Seraman is gone!"

"Gone?"

"Yes, Saladin of Slaughter and Dread," said the panting guard.

"Calm yourself," Mazlund said, smiling.

Good, he thought, Seraman may think that he is defecting. Actually, he becomes my messenger, particularly since Neutralon seems unwilling to agree to my humble proposal.

"Help yourself to wine," Mazlund said, waving an arm toward a flagon. The guard's hand trembled as he poured some Chablis into a tumbler.

"It taught me point of view, " Cybella said.

"I think I understand," said Grunius.

"As spirit of the tree, I experienced myself through the reach of the tree into the spring. I could tremble on the edge of each new leaf. I could touch the roots as they threaded past the stones in search of water. I could feel the rings at the tree's center forming their measurement of the years. They were neither slow nor fast, just a fact of nature. And now, I do not observe the water or the clouds. I am the observation. It is not a matter of my being here and something else being there. I deny the separation."

"I grasp the concept," Grunius said.

"But you must also observe the separation."

"Yes. I must translate what I see into language. That involves a process of abstraction and of interpretation."

"I would think that the interpretation would be the most difficult."

"It is. My own subjective point of view comes into play."

"And you befriend it?"

"I try. I now have the following to interpret, a combination of

97

cloud-shape, leaves against the sunset, and the stars that splash from the Dipper:

> The way the light shines down
> upon the ground
> will tell you when to wait,
> and thus decide your fate."

"And how do you deconstruct that one?" Cybella asked.
"I don't know."
"Perhaps you will know when the actual sight presents itself."
"Perhaps. But will that be in time?"
"The summer draws on. My clematis are out."
"Those purple flowers?"
"Yes."
"The earth will soon begin to give up its heat, and that means we reach conclusions."
"No doubt." She paused. "I wonder what they will be."

Estrella and Umgalla looked into the fire, dropping now into the pure gold of the last embers.
"We dance and sing around a fire," Umgalla said.
"But that does not..." Estrella said.
"We know that. It does not bring god down to us. We are sure he or she pays little attention to all that commotion. It is a community event. We enjoy it. And it reminds us of our contact with that power in the sky. We cannot make it come again by our dance and song. Perhaps our ancestors did believe in that version of magic. But we know that it will return, just at the point when it seems to have forsaken the sky."
"Faith."
"Yes," Umgalla said.
"We share that, do we not?"
"Apparently, we do. Your story is about a young man who was nailed to a tree?"
"Yes."
"It will take me some time. But the concept of giving oneself for

others is not foreign to our culture. Once, of course, my own people sacrificed animals to the great god in the sky."

"And the central event of our system of belief was a sacrifice."

"A human sacrifice. Your God did ask a lot, did he not?"

"He did."

"I think the problem is this emphasis on guilt. I do not live a guilt-free life. No one does. But I prefer not to dwell on it. I prefer not to think of myself as miserable merely because I cannot sacrifice myself as your young God did. We are hardly a mistake-free species. One could become paralyzed by guilt."

"Yes. I think you do define a valid issue."

"My people are bronze – the color that the sun has given us. We know that we are not just of nature, that our ability to think removes us from nature to some extent. But we also believe in a oneness with nature. It is somewhat like what you call symbiosis. We are not sure – I am not, at least – that we need an intermediary. We can read the trees as they move with the wind and the sky as it reshapes itself above the farthest hillsides and the silence before thunder."

"Yes, and the silence after. I can understand that."

"Is there room enough...?"

"For two ways of believing in God? Oh yes. We have among us those who still believe in many gods. The good of the community depends on our willingness to let others believe as they will. Our stories have intersected, not collided. Otherwise..."

"Yes, you would doom yourselves and all ways of believing in God."

"Or not believing, as the case might be."

Neutralon realized that he was watched, particularly after his recent conferences with Mazlund. He was treated with respect by Mazlund's household staff – he had, after all, been a Prince of Archerland – but he was aware that from spy-holes in walls and through cracks where floors met ceilings, he was constantly observed. And he could tell that Mazlund was making preparations for war. Neutralon did not have much time.

And so, as he had so seldom in the past, he took a chance. He slipped from his chamber one evening. He had given the two guards a flagon of wine and told them that he was retiring. The wine had done its work.

How would he get past the guards at the door below?

"Mazlund wants all guards in his council chamber immediately!"

"But we must keep certain guards at their posts!"

"I have my orders. You have yours."

Mazlund was puzzled to see his entire security staff file into his chamber.

"What are you doing here?"

"You sent for us, Viscount of Cruelty and Vindictiveness!"

Had he?

"Yes. You have grown too lax. I want you to redouble your efforts! That is all."

The Captain of the Guard thumped his chest, about faced, and marched, the other following in a column of twos.

But the lock was rusty. Just as Neutralon was about to give up and face the issue of his phony order to the guard – how would he explain that? – the lock snapped open, flaking rust across the back of his hand. He heard the guard's boots on the stone of the passageway behind him. Sweating into his silken tunic, Neutralon slipped through the door to the Underworld.

After Umgalla had returned to his encampment, Estrella sat thinking by the murmuring embers.

We are far from that other land, Estrella thought. It is not just the physical distance. When young Paul set out from Tidal Plain, witches existed who could cast spells and almost convince Paul to step over a precipice into a snake-infested swamp. Only his dog, Major, as the story goes, had saved him from that final step with a warning bark. Paul had been enchanted by a beautiful princess and had almost been charmed from his mission. A sea-monster, Raptalemon, had almost defeated young Paul in the Grottoes near Enclava. It had been a close thing! And had Mazlund not told his guards not to interfere no matter what they heard, Paul would not have defeated him in that chamber to which Paul had come, unbeknownst to the over-confident Ruler of the Undernature. Mazlund's guards laughed, albeit uneasily, at their commander's frantic yelps for help, convinced that Mazlund was merely testing them. And Mazlund had been forced to reshape himself into the form of a ferocious black dog and had almost succeeded in defeating Paul as the Black Palace burned around them, the flames seeping toward the room where the combat raged. Major had died in that battle. Mazlund had been able to reconstitute himself from the marrow of a bone fragment that had been all that was left of the black dog. It had been a different world, a world of charms and giants and spirits of glen and grove, as Cybella had been, and of isolated trolls who had lived under bridges, like Tomaso, now a loyal servant of what was left of Archerland. The new world in which they lived now, Estrella thought, still contained evil. That was a constant. But it was a subtle thing, this evil, often hard to recognize, often seemingly the more attractive of two alternatives, often lurking inside the unsuspecting person who was convinced that he or she was incapable of it – until that person looked back in horror upon what he or she had done. Was that old world a more frightening place, as the old stories seemed to say? Estrella did not think so! It was still a place where "almost" seemed to rule.

But whatever she thought, it was time for sleep, and the reinvigoration of dreaming.

"If we could capture their Queen..." Mazlund mused. "Neutralon has disappeared. Somewhere in the Fortress, I am told. But I have no confidence in his helping us with any formal arrangement. We must seize Glorimere."

"What then?" Langar asked.

"We would be in a position to bargain."

"For what?"

"I want merely to control this space." Mazlund held his arms wide. "The fortress and its contiguous area."

"They would see you as a threat."

"Perhaps. But we could negotiate a treaty."

"They would not believe you, Mazlund. You have torn up so many treaties in the past. Your non-proliferation of crossbows agreement. But that proved counterproductive when Archerland increased its production of the long bow. You will recall the Battle of the Watermeadows."

Mazlund scowled.

"Your promise not to use poisonous smoke in battle," Langar

continued. "You will recall what happened when the wind shifted as you were about to charge the retreating enemy on the road from Corilus to the Castle of Peace."

Mazlund opened his mouth, but said nothing.

"Not everyone forgets the past," Langar said.

"That is an inconvenience, I admit."

"Memory can be a guide to present action," Langar said.

"Are you on my side or not?" Mazlund snapped.

"On yours, of course, Great Gremlin of Grim Night."

"Gremlin?"

"Would you want your followers to accede to plans that might explode in your face? I merely point out that your signature on a treaty is hardly a guarantee, particularly to those like Estrella who have fought against you in the field."

"So? What is on your mind?"

"I agree that capturing the Queen could be a benefit. But I would suggest..."

Langar paused.

"What?"

"That in some way we use the Queen – assuming that we can capture her – as a lure, a way of leading the others into a trap."

"Good! Tell me how?"

"I am thinking of the downside here."

"If you must. What is the downside."

"We cannot be sure that the others would lift a hand in defense of Glorimere. She betrayed them, after all."

"A small betrayal in the middle distance. So what?"

"To you, for whom betrayal is second nature, not much, I agree. For Archerland, her defection from King Mark meant a civil war. Or, at least, my brother thought so at the time. For you, for whom civil war is a desideratum, that may mean little."

"But it does to them. Yes, I concede your point. Still..."

"Yes. She may have won their favor. Clearly, she has been accepted into their camp, however grudgingly that embrace may be."

"Yes, yes. What is your plan? As I have told you, if this succeeds, she is yours. Here with my army ready, horses straining at the reins, I am still reluctant to rely on mere battle. I still want something more certain."

"So I understand, Emir of Evil. You have lost so often in the past. Here, then, is my plan ."

Estrella had one of those dreams in which the structure of the entire cosmos is opened to the dreamer. She saw the skies, where dragonish clouds cavorted around the blue-gray castles and temples that towered in great cities down over the horizon. She saw the fertile plains of Archerland and the white rivers that tumbled over rocks to intersect the plain as plants rose between the windrows and worked their way to fruition. Along the pathways, she met Killbeard and Evalinda, and two kings named Paul, and Queen Aprilla, and Princess Juna, and Kermath. She exchanged smiles and a word with each, as if they were out for a stroll in the mild air. A great white dog frisked up to her. She leaned down to stroke the smooth coat beneath is throat. "Hello, Major!" she said. She looked for George – she was aware of that in her dream – but she did not find him. She wandered this burgeoning zone until she came upon the opening to a zone below the earth. Although she could not see down into it, she could tell that this area was as vast as the earth itself. From it came the cries of man and animal. That was a place to avoid! It woke her up. Only a dream, she said to herself, recalling the more reassuring images of her inner adventure. Still, she carried the sounds coming from that great fissure with her as she embarked on her day.

Neutralon stared along the floor of a cool, dank tunnel.

Approaching him was a tall man in bronze armor. A gleaming helmet with a nose-plate attached rose with a plume above his head.

"I fear I have kept you waiting," Neutralon said.

"Time means nothing here. You bring it with you. You also bring that dimension known as distance. Come, we have a walk ahead of us!"

As they walked, the warrior spoke.

"When I was above the ground, my name was Hector."

"I know the name."

"You do?"

"Yes, the story of your city is well known to us. I am afraid that it is a cautionary tale."

"Yes, it must be. Nothing is good in that story, even for the Greeks, the winners. They began the war with an atrocity – the sacrifice of Agamemnon's daughter – and they ended it with deceit. Of course, I was not there at the end. I came out of the battle one evening, lay my sword and my eagle-crested shield aside, and bathed my body in a tributary of the Scimander. Bruises from the blows against my armor – they hurt more than actual wounds. Achilles was in the field that day, furious at the death of his friend, Patroclus. Achilles and his Mirmidons – a nasty group that! – came upon me. I offered to meet him in single combat and asked him – without cowering – to forego his advantage. They set upon me. Then Achilles tied what was left of me to his chariot and pulled me through the dust around the walls of Troy. I could do nothing when the Greeks pretended to flee and left that horse. Cassandra warned them. But no one heeds a mad woman. Loacoon told them that the great horse had a Greekish stink to it. But a sea monster took him into the water, and the people were fearful of Posiedon. My shade drifted helplessly amid the brief debate. "Bring this carven horse to Athena's shrine," the people shouted, pulling away the stones of the wall to make room for the passage of the thing. The horse was pulled inside. The people celebrated and drank their wine, posted drowsy guards, and went home to bed, dreaming of the quiet days ahead. And then, an hour before the birds began to summon the light again from the east, the Greeks let down a ladder from the belly of the horse and fell upon the sentries slumbering, their heads on their hands over their spears. And dawn's fire was pale compared to the flames that consumed our city that morning. My soul wandered baffled for days amid the crystal cinders until they buried me, along with all those who died that night. Scarcely enough people came down from the hills after they had fled to do the job. Aeneas had fled, of course, with Anchises on his back, and Hecuba, and my wife, Andromache, had been taken prisoner by the Greeks. And I am a guide in this Afterworld."

"It is a sad tale."

"Yes, and it was a fault regardless of the horse. I could have persuaded Priam to give Helen back to Menelaus. The war that followed – all those who died in it – was for nothing!"

They came a widening and then saw the place Estrella had described to him, an island surrounded by water. But it was not water so much as it was music, a drifting melody that rose and fell between the place where he stood and the island beyond. This is like being in a dream, he thought. Time and place shift so quickly that I, the dreamer, am lost!

"Step in the boat," Hector said.

Yes, there was a small boat seeming to float the mist in front of him.

"Careful! It is unaccustomed to weight."

Yes, he brought weight with him as well.

"I leave you now," Hector said.

"Farewell Hector, Tamer of Horses!"

The tall man turned and walked away, but his armor made no sound as he left.

Neutralon took the single paddle and made his way through the mist. The boat, having never held more than the weight of a shade, sloshed down to its gunnels. Gingerly, he landed on the island.

"I come to..."

"We know your mission!"

This was said by two voices, a woman's and a man's in perfect unison, like the voices of a well-trained chorus. They were a duet.

"Silence! Listen!"

> "You have arrived from up above.
> You do not have to say.
> You come to us from those we love,
> Who have lost their way.
>
> They seek to learn about their fate.
> And if you should get back,
> Tell them they must learn to wait,
> Not hasten to attack."

The island faded, as if two great hands had rubbed the mist across its surface. The music folded up within the disappearance.

The boat was gone, but so was the water.

If I get back... Neutralon thought.

I must find the door again. And, this time, it will be guarded. How will I get past those guards and bring my message to the survivors of Archerland? It had not been the getting here that was difficult, he realized. It will be the going back!

"No!" Estrella said. "This is our quarrel. You people have lived here in peace for generations. Do not endanger yourselves by taking sides. If we lose, you lose."

"You said it correctly," Umgalla replied.

"What do you mean?"

"I mean that if you lose, we lose. Do not think that the evil man..."

"Not a man!"

"Whatever he is, do not believe that he will let us live in our lands in peace. He is a destroyer of people, an enemy of peace."

"But, Umgalla, we have fought him before when it seemed that we were hopelessly outnumbered."

"And that is a reason why you should not accept more help? How many times in the past have you raised your eyes to the pathway behind you hoping to see above the trees the dust of a column coming to reinforce your lines?"

She had to admit that she had done that often enough, although she tried never to betray the desperation in her eyes as she did so. That was seldom a confidence-builder for her troops.

"Even so," she said, "we should fight this battle alone."

"Not so, Estrella. We share this common enemy. If we do not fight him together, he will destroy us separately. It is that simple."

"Take it to your people. Ask them."

"I have."

"So you come here with their consent."

"I would not come here otherwise. I could not."

Mazlund leaned over the scale model that Reeps, his designer, had prepared for him.

Yes, yes, Mazlund thought, inwardly rubbing his hands together, this will outdo the Temple of Solomon! Mazlund had seen that once from afar. I, too, will have perfect stones fitted together, so that no sound of chisel or mallet will intrude on my reverie. I, too, will have the place surrounded by cedar trees, with olive groves spreading over the hills and out of sight, and vines growing in the clay of south-looking hillsides to be crushed, in their time, into wine. I will have a great cauldron of brass, held on the shoulders of twelve great bulls, three each looking at each of the four major compass points. That will suggest the outgoing azimuths of the world that I control. I will have golden candlesticks, as Solomon did, and a fountain rising in the central courtyard. And above the fountain will be a marble statue of me! On horseback, of course, if we can find enough marble.

His own followers grumbled and groused when he put them to work. They had grown soft with their easy rounds of guard duty and their ample rations of wine. But they could be overseers. He would impress the natives. They had been slaves before. Their ancestral mentality would make it easy for Mazlund to make them slaves again. They had inherited the attitude, although they would not know that until Mazlund made it clear to them. Perhaps they had inherited the gene, as well. Here, Mazlund's knowledge of science met its limits. Juna would have known! Ah well, power dictated reality.

"We will begin with the banquet hall," Mazlund said.

"Very good, Dread Decider of Destiny," Reeps said, bowing.

But Mazlund had a thought. Suppose Lucifer, whom I have not seen in several millenia, decides that he likes this magnificence that I have caused to be created here in this desert place? He outranks me!

The thought ruined his day.

"Chirac, wine!"

And when Chirac had brought a decanter of dry white wine imported from a distant river valley when the Conquistadors had inhabited the Fortress, Mazlund said, "Leave the bottle."

Chirac, offended at the implied insult to a fine vintage, turned and left the chamber.

Neutralon rushed back along the pathway, although it did not seem to be the same one he had taken to come into this place. It never is in dreams, he thought. Their cartographer is a madman! He did not dare to look to the left or right. And then he came to a vast plain swept with a shifting wind. On it banners pulled back and forth in that confused air, and frenzied human shapes chased one and then abandoned that to run after another. All the flags were the same, a bland white banner without a symbol.

"You who prefer neutrality! Join your fellows! These many whom death has undone did not choose when they were above the earth. And now they cannot!"

Neutralon took a step toward one of the many groups rushing restlessly across this huge space. He had lost sight of the pathway.

"No!" he said, shaking free of whatever tugged at him. "I have chosen!"

The narrow path threaded before him again. He walked, head held high, down the many miles of the space of shifting winds.

Neutralon knew that Mazlund wanted only Glorimere as the price of peace between the remnants of Archerland and the Darkforce. And Glorimere had been disgraced in the world before this one, the cause of a fatal rift between King Mark and his most trusted Lieutenant, Linvallen. Was Hector's story of Helen meant to be a precedent?

How would Neutralon know?

XII.

Mazlund stood on the parapet, gazing out at the valley, the river that ran at its heart, and at the wooded hills beyond. He took a sip of some of that splendid Medoc that had not turned to vinegar, as the bitter von Rodent had wished. I command all that I survey, he thought. But, more than that, I have come at last to a zone free of that interfering deity of theirs! He could not use the "G" word, of course.

Long ago, although it still corroded in his memory like cobalt, he had managed to cleave a small piece of land from the mainland, a place on which he could stand alone and wage his war against their deity, profanity on his lips if he called Him by name. He had for an instant become an independent evil and from that small beginning Mazlund would be able to grow and prosper, creating a kingdom equal to and competitive with that other all-reaching zone that included even Mazlund within it. But the instant that he had taken a deep breath, absorbing the delicious foulness of his own atmosphere, a cloud had formed and from it had reached the column of a rainbow. The colors had touched his island and the mainland, and then had arched above, spliced a spectacular spectrum across the sky, and pulled the two pieces of land, the large and the small, together again. Mazlund had been reminded of the promise that his competitor had made long before, just after his friend Lucifer had persuaded those two to enjoy the enticing fruit and after Mazlund himself had gone on a tour that ultimately necessitated that flood. He recalled his conversation with Noah.

"What has He given you – a lot of work to be performed under a burning sun as the sweat of your brow drops your precious salt into the ground?"

"We must work," Noah had replied. "It has been decreed since our ancestors of recent memory ignored His prohibition. I do not complain about the work. My fields and vineyards are not merely mine. They will be passed on to many generations."

"But I will make it easier for you in your approaching old age."

"Yes, husband," Mrs. Noah had said. "Listen to him. You cannot work forever."

"That I know, wife. But I choose to follow the dictates of the Living Lord."

Mazlund winced.

"That sort of talk has gone out of fashion," he said.

"Fashion? It comes and goes," Noah had replied. "The Living Lord lives on."

"Well, if you will have a look at these brochures. I'll leave them with you."

Mazlund handed them to Mrs. Noah.

"Thank you. I'll make sure that he reads them," she said.

Noah had snatched them from her hand and tossed them into the fire, where they burned with the hissing characteristic of green wood.

But that, Mazlund thought, had been in a place pervaded with the presence of their inconvenient deity.

He took a sip of wine and rolled it around his tongue and let it rest along his palate before he swallowed it.

This place is mine. Mine alone!

To test that thesis he uttered an imprecation that ruffled the bracken nearby.

He waited.

He laughed at the distant rumble of thunder. Merely the voice of cumulous building up as the heat of day begins to rise into the moisture that had been gathering since noon on all horizons.

No need to build a simulated nature here. Grunius had built a world under Archerland, simulating the original in all ways. It had been like the reflection in a perfect mirror. But a mirror is not reality, as we discover, Mazlund knew, when we rush to embrace ourselves. It had gone wrong when, through a confusion in a chemical formulation, the falling leaves of a pseudo-autumn had become rabid bats that fortunately had driven themselves mad before they could become marauders. They had dived in perfect formation into an empty swamp.

"We overestimated the acidic content," Grunius had explained.

"How could you do that?" Mazlund had demanded.

"Nature is a delicate balance, Progenitor of Pain. In this case, we needed bats, but our sample came from bats accustomed to an acid-thin soil. We simply overcompensated. They did not have time to evolve toward a compensatory status."

"Evolve?"

"Yes, Prince of Perversity. We tried to match the evolutionary cycle of each species. Of course, that process was imprecise at best. We cannot always imitate a rhythm of a much more subtle construction than ours."

"But..."

"For example, Sultan of Nasty Surprises, we could not hope to simulate the original six day process. That would have called for the intervention of..."

"Don't say that word!"

And, of course, other mishaps had occurred. A race of carnivorous trees had one day attacked a hubris of lions, resulting in a roaring and rending that had awakened Mazlund from a nap and that had torn a hole in the recently implanted fabric that Grunius and his artisans had taken weeks to complete by slow crocheting. Some lions had fled and had become vegetarians in revenge. Some trees had been clawed down. Others were licking their leaves and daring beasts of the field to enter their deceptive shade. None did and the zone became a stunted wasteland in a few weeks.

One of Grunius's rivers had caught fire.

"Too much oxygen," he had explained.

Neutalon stood on the other side of the great door. Even through the thick oaken slabs held together by heavy iron flanges he could hear the restless shuffle of boots and the thump of spear-ends on the stone floor.

A wisp of the land he had left trailed behind him. That land had held threats, of course, but what he remembered was the music, as if it still sounded to the person waking from a dream.

"Come music!" he whispered.

He stood aside. The wisp of sound brushed against the thickness of the door then curled back toward the depths of the Afterworld.

"Go through!" Neutralon said. "Be for once like my own sight that can go through surfaces and see a future come into being!"

The music paused and became a cloud of sound gathering along the splinters and knots of the ancient door.

Neutralon held his arms above the quivering chords.

And then they moved like smoke along the door and infiltrated the veins of wood and rippled above the iron fixtures and pulled the wisp after them, with the sound of water sinking into earth after rain.

The great door began to open along the deep gouges of white granite that it had worn over time in the stone.

Neutralon stood aside.

The two guards, like ponies seeking their barn, rushed past, pursuing the creep of music down the stony path to the Underworld.

Neutralon was soon up the corridor and into the secret room overlooking the moat. Before moonrise he would be on the other side. He must get to his countrymen as soon as possible. And he knew that they must not surrender Glorimere. Helen had been one thing. Holding on to her brought down the shrines and citadels of Illium. But to surrender Glorimere, regardless of her past defections, would be the beginning of the end of what was left of Archerland. And, that intangible factor still might hold. That Living Lord might still look down on the survivors from His inscrutable sky with a favorable eye. Neutralon uttered a brief prayer as he circled through the forest toward his friends.

He prayed that he would get there in time. And, as his final clause, he prayed that he would know what to do when he got there. That was a lot to ask in one prayer!

Estrella looked across at Mazlund's Blackforce, three units lined up in perfect formation, a left flank, a center, and a right flank, pennants flicking in the morning wind, horses pulling against the reins, great eyes rolling back toward their masters, eager for the command of "Charge!" and the bugle call that would summon their power into a collective and overpowering thrust, punctuated with the lash of sabers above the great equine bulk of the army's motive power. The black banners would hold against the wind at the end of the battle, merging with the shadows of sunset. And it would be the sun falling on what was left of Archerland.

Where is Umgalla? She cast a glance behind her, trying not to convey anxiety. Had he, at the last minute, decided that she had been right, that the cause of those who had survived the erasure of Archerland was not that of the native inhabitants of this land? If so, she could not blame him. They would survive. Still, she wished that he and his warriors were here. If she were to lead a charge, a volley or two of arrows into the enemy was a precondition to her success. If not, the charge would amount to a gallant mass suicide. It might anyway. What was left of Archerland – all the history, the adventures of those who had believed in it, the memory of its towers and temples and people – would lie with eyes open and reflecting the blankness of an uncaring sky upon that field. The alternative – to be slaves, helping Mazlund build whatever it was he was constructing in that further valley, next to the Fortress he had inherited from the prior invaders of this land. Estrella shook her head. No. Better battle and its more-than-likely outcome than that!

Across from Estrella and her small band, Mazlund used his single eye to focus the lens on his telescope.

"We could have swept them from the field," he said. "We did not need your subtle device."

"Perhaps not, Vindictive Viceroy," Langar replied. "I admit that they are a pathetic group, a few lean horses, weapons more prone to ferric oxide than to effective use in battle, and an overall aura of hopelessness. One is surprised to find them assembled there! Still, why take chances?"

But Mazlund knew that his own careful stratagems in the past had resulted in disaster when put to the test.

"I would rather meet them in battle, in the close-in shock of a good cavalry charge!"

Langar had been in battle. He was not a coward.

"The problem with battle, Potentate of Pure Terror, is that you introduce the law of unintended consequences."

How well Mazlund knew that!

"Better go with a sure thing," Langar said.

"Look!" Mazlund said, pointing across the valley.

"Yes. Umgalla and those savages are joining them."

Mazlund brushed away a shadow of foreboding with his right hand.

"All the better," he said. "I can dispatch two enemies in a single action this way. I would have to go after those natives sooner or later.

Now, they save me the time and trouble. What can their puny arrows do to us? Good! Good!"

"We have come at this time to join you against a common enemy, but primarily because you are our friends. We do not desert our friends," Umgalla said.

"I am glad you are here," Estrella replied.

Still, she thought, this merely gives Mazlund a chance to dispatch both of his enemies in one encounter. Look at the force opposing us across the valley! No! These are just the thoughts that invariably inhabit commanders before a battle. And inhibit them. Doubt. Even fear. But she knew that those traitors deserted once the fight was joined. They fled with the first bugle call.

"Yes," she said, "we will need your most accurate arrows to fly across this valley. And, under them, we will mount our charge."

"No!" Glorimere twisted the horse's head, pulling the reins from Gregg's hands. She kicked her feet into the side of Icarus and charged toward the enemy lines.

Von Beak and von Rodent were in command of the right and left flanks of Mazlund's small army. Mazlund stood in front of the center force, with Langar by his side. They watched as Glorimere detached herself from the tiny band of Archerland survivors and native Oldlanders and was chased by a funnel of dust down the hill.

"Will the others follow?" Mazlund wondered aloud.

"Let us hope so, Trireme of Terror."

"Trireme?"

"A mighty vessel."

"Well..."

Mazlund did not think of himself as a vessel, mighty or otherwise. A negative cornucopia? Perhaps. No! That meant that he had a feminine side, as waggish theorists postulated, and that thesis Mazlund vehemently denied. The only feminine side he recognized was that of his arachnid self. When he chose – sometimes very suddenly – to become a spider, he was wary of the lady spiders. He was respectful, of course, but he kept his distance.

Neutralon, having circled to the south now came upon the combined forces of Archerland and Umgalla from their right. He saw Glorimere's gallop down the hillside.

I am too late! he thought. They will follow her!

"She has stopped," Langar said.

"Daring us to capture her."

Mazlund held both arms up, palms backward. He pushed his arms back, to dissuade any movement from his flanks.

"Yes," Mazlund said. "And the others are about to follow her! Good! Good!"

But von Beak and von Rodent, each eager for the approval of the Master of Malevolence, saw only the upraised arms about, they inferred, to be thrust forward. Each commander waved his sword against the clouds and charged to a simultaneous blatting of bugles. What glory it would be to bring the once-Queen of Archerland back as prisoner. The Order of the Black Spider dangled itself in front of each of their eyes as the air rushed past them. Down the hillside they went, their battalions following.

Gregg was no horseman, but he put his foot into the stirrup of the horse that Umgalla had given him. Before he could swing up, Neutralon pulled his shoulder.

"I must go after her!"

The mounted force behind him prepared to follow.

"No!" Neutralon said.

Gregg's powerful arms twisted away from Neutralon's frail grip. But this time Grunius pulled him down and held him for a moment.

"Yes," said Grunius. "I see it too! The way their armor glints against that cloud and reflects against that grassy area in the valley. I can read it! Stay, Gregg!"

Cybella had joined Neutralon and Grunius.

"No!" she cried. "I see the meaning in that shadow of the moon – what is and isn't there! Stop, Gregg!"

Gregg could easily have wrested free of the combined grip of Grunius and Neutralon, and of Cybella clasping one of his knees – his arms and shoulders had lifted traps and nets from the resisting ocean and his legs had thickened against the consistent back-and-forth of the deck of his boat – but Estrella rushed forward.

"Yes, Gregg," she said quietly. "Stop."

He heard the authority in her voice.

Gregg's shoulders slumped as he looked down the hillside at Glorimere, now pausing at the bottom of the valley.

The horsemen and women behind Gregg reached forward to pat and soothe their horses, ready an instant before to charge across the valley at the army that faced them.

"No!" shouted Mazlund.

"No!" shouted Langar.

Each spurred his own horse forward in an effort to head off the chargers of their flanking battalions.

Here, Langar's plan came into play. He had had a deep pit constructed, in darkness, and covered with a net and a thin planting of grass. The extra dirt had been dumped near a construction site on the south wall of the Fortress, where Mazlund was building his new banquet hall. Everything between the two hillsides resembled a meadow, a suitable site for the collision of even the paltry army on one side and the formidable force on the other that faced each other across its expanse.

Glorimere had stopped just in front of the concealed pit. Now, von Beak and von Rodent, and, for that matter, Mazlund and Langer – the only two who knew of the trap that had been set for the rival force – charged toward it.

"Stop, you fools!" Mazland shouted to the left and right.

Ah, he wants all the glory for himself, von Rodent thought, watching the wilding gesticulating Mazlund, but not hearing his command. Von Rodent spurred the harder.

He can't bear to share the honor of this capture, von Beak thought, interpreting Mazlund's words, which von Beak could hear, as Mazlund's effort to get in front of his commanders. I'll show him!

Each commander day-dreamed – in a quick image, of course – of the elegant decoration that would hang from his throat after this action was completed. He'll *have* to give it to me, each one shouted to himself, digging iron spurs into his horse's haunch.

The valley echoed with thunder as if it were beneath a giant storm cloud. Mazlund looked behind him. His own force was at the heels of his great charger, Winter Kreig, the wild horse he had trained as his own. Mazlund realized that they could not stop!

He saw Langar's eyes beside him roll white in panic.

The earth on either side of the pit collapsed, and horse and rider twisted as hooves could find no place to plant themselves. The eyes of the horses turned into their sockets. Their riders stared at emptiness.

Glorimere saw the earth below her horse's head begin to cake and fall. Her horse tried to back, but found no place for his forefeet. Glorimere looked up. Yes! The Darkforce was charging toward this great crevasse. She would take them with her! She wished that Linvallen, her lost warrior, could see her now!

Finding himself atumble, Mazlund made a snap decision.

"D'Nulzam!"

He became a spider, floating free of his plunging charger and tossing a filament toward the side of the chasm. It caught. Mazlund swung back and forth for an instant, almost getting plonked by a falling horse and rider of his cavalry. Then he scuttled rapidly up the thread he had extruded and out of the way. The chaos and confusion of falling bodies caused the side of the great hole to tremble, but Mazlund held firm, hoping that he had not attached himself to a chunk that would come loose in this shaking chaos. It had seemed like such a plausible concept when Langar had set it forth!

When his horse skidded over the edge of the deep hole that Langar had constructed, Langar knew it was too late. He was ashamed of his momentary panic. Too bad, he thought, this was a good horse. Is a good horse, he corrected, for an instant more. He smiled at himself. He mourned the horse? Yes, if he loved anything beside himself, he loved the handsome brown horse with the star on its forehead. He saw Mazlund, now a spider, clinging to the edge of the fissure. That's too bad too! I picked the wrong side, he thought. But he had no regrets. He would have shrugged had he not been falling head over heel toward the bottom of the chasm, where horses and Mazlund's human followers were beginning to pile up. Panicky shouts grew louder as he fell, but Langar laughed. That beautiful horse had dropped away below him. He thought of Native Star flicking a fly from its rear flank as if that flank were part of a separate animal. For himself? Not a tear. But for that lovely animal...

Mazlund scuttled on many legs away from the great fissure in the earth that he and Langar had prepared for the survivors of Archerland. His tiny spider brain vibrated with a combination of rage and alarm at yet another close call. What had gone wrong? He lacked the neurons to arrive at an answer. A female spider came toward him, eyes glinting in welcome. Mazlund's spider brain thought quickly and, just as quickly, the black legs and plinth-like body had expanded into the black fur that covered the veins and ribs of a rat. Mazlund waved his brand-new black tail. The female spider, disappointed and alarmed, crept into a crack in the disturbed ground in which the remnants of Mazlund's cavalry still flailed feebly. In their final throes, if you will, Mazlund thought. I will, Mazlund's rat-brain continued. I have no choice. When did I last have a choice? When I chose not to, he thought. His rat-ears wiggled as they heard a hoofbeat. I can choose to be a crow, he thought. And so he became one. His crow-brain hissed with frustration as he flapped off, zeroing-in on the underbrush with his single keen black eye for something dead on which to feast.

A few survivors scratched out of the great cavity as rats, or scurried away on many legs as spiders, or climbed with a crack of wings as crows, their shoulders creaking like the spars of ships in wind, their "Crowl! Crowl!" a sound of the panic that a near-miss had induced. These refugees joined in a remote corner of the mainland to form a cell, the crows on branches, the rats squirming below, the spiders clambering onto hastily spun webs. They looked for the moment like a collection of scavengers, bearers of plague, and poisoners, meeting for a malign convention away from any human eyes. It always exists, that evil possibility, even if out of sight. And Mazlund, alert from long experience to the dangers that the aftermath of battle may hold, ducked into the cover of the forest, almost pranging against an oak as he did so. How he missed his depth perception! He surveyed his diminished army with a single, disapproving eye, some of the survivors still in the guises of the rats, spiders, and crows that had escaped the squashing of the pit, and decided that he would stay out of sight for the time being, perhaps a millenium or two.

His decision to take to the woods was rewarded as he watched the Eagle Squadron swoop down upon the hapless rats who had stayed in the open too long.

He looked over this ragtag band of survivors. The vons – Beak and Rodent – had made it, but they would not meet his eye. He did not have to say anything. They had scuttled his master plan. He would deal with them when time served. He looked forward to snapping their field-marshal batons over his knee and tossing the remnants into the woodpile. He had been a fool to promote them just before this non-battle! A fool? No one else had dare say so, he said to himself.

His crow-brain touched the dim, outward circle of memory he needed.

"D'Nulzam!"

Soon, he was standing in his human disguise again. He reached inside his tunic for his eyepatch and its ribbon and pulled the ribbon down to his ears. Yes, better! Had he gotten so accustomed to disaster that he could just stand there? Apparently. Something is to be said, he thought, for experience. But what?

He saw a spider sidle toward him. Vallarte! Yes, he recognized that particular gleam of eye. Vallarte must be unable to make the transformation back to arrogant, bemedalled hussar, Mazlund thought. Well, let him stew for a while. That will teach him some humility! He will owe me! Mazlund turned away from the pleading spider, but Mazlund failed to see the female spider insinuating her way across the pine needles.

"All right, Vallarte," Mazlund said, turning back to where the spider had been.

But the spider was gone. Mazlund shuddered for an instant. He himself had only a moment ago chosen that guise wherein to make his own escape. While Mazlund was often terrified at the thought of his own immortality, he did not harbor any wish to test that thesis against its alternative. All these contradictions! he grumbled to himself. How is a fallen angel to make sense of anything!

To Raise Another World

"That, Mazlund, is the point!" said a voice he vaguely recognized.

The earth on either side of the cavity that Langar had caused to be dug weakened and tumbled in. The hillsides between trembled. Estrella held a constraining arm against Gregg, who had taken a step forward.

Far above the land, a city of cumulous castles rose. The sun, falling away, illuminated the top-most clouds in blue, and green, and orange.

How beautiful is God's creation, Estrella thought, looking westward. And how fragile!

Mazlund surveyed the battlefield with his single eye from behind a copse of myrrh trees. The cauldron of the abyss had quieted down. Good – what an awful racket that had been! The band composed of Archerland survivors and Umgalla's tribe still stood on the opposite hillside. Mazlund attempted to think of what his revenge would be. It would have no bounds. But this effort at conceptualization was interrupted by words he could recall from the history that had flowed outward from his rebellion, with Lucifer, against that power he could not name. The words seemed to come from inside his mind!

> "And Daniel dreamed. And in that dream, a voice
> condemned the King of Babylon, and said,
> 'Nebuchadnezzar, thou shall eat the grass
> that beasts consume, and your very hair
> shall be like feathers of the eagle, and
> the nails of your hands shall be the claws
> of birds, for your greatness is like a tree that climbs
> to heaven high. It shall be cut, and you
> will fall, until you raise your eyes again,
> and understand where everlasting rule
> resides, and dominion over all below.'"

Mazlund glanced at the hair on his arm. That arm had been a wing and had lately felt the sharpness of feathers growing there, stinging outward from the bone. His hands had been like the claws of a bird clasping the branch of a larch, a crow to be precise. But he would not raise his single eye and accept that power. He had come close this time to ruling a land from which that power had been exiled. That field was lost, but others would open along the long perspective of history and time that lay ahead.

Mazlund gazed on the bright clouds catching an angle of afternoon sun and swelling like the rarest of marble above him against a vastness of blue. The wind-carved city reminded him only that he would not inhabit the magnificent palace he had planned. Its model would remain in the Fortress, and he would be mocked by those who found it. Blast!

Neutralon approached Estrella.

"Since Kermath died, shortly before Archerland itself was no more, we have not had a spiritual leader."

"I know," Estrella said. "Like all our ancestors, Kermath lies buried in the buried land. And we have needed such a man."

"You will think me bold, but I have learned much since I came to you so short a time ago. I have learned that my fate is woven to yours and that yours is part of a larger fabric – the metaphor fails me – that exists on a loom that was constructed before we were and whose warp and woof will outlast us by more time than it has existed so far."

"Yes, my own belief in what you say has been restored here in this place. People were here to help us even before we came. Nature itself was accepting of us. We did not land on icy rocks in the depth of winter, with only wind and snow to welcome us. Something more was at work. And I say that knowing that some who still believed did not survive the flood that washed over our motherland."

"What I ask, Estrella, is simple. Still, you may deny me and I will not be angry."

"And what is it you would have?"

"I would like to be the one who offers prayers."

"As Kermath did?"

"I cannot take his place. The man was infused with the spirit and he could put it into words. But as I find the words, I also feel an opening between where I stand and something else – not just above me, but below me, and around me. I would like to phrase that feeling for our people."

"Since you have been called by that power that you sense, of course. You can be the one who says the prayers for our community."

Neutralon was overjoyed and did not trust himself to reply. He nodded.

"Now, a time of peace," Gregg said.

"Peace? I doubt it," Estrella said. "Not in this world. Mazlund continues to work. And, as we often notice, the Mazlund-in-us is at work."

She paused to glance at her sons. Their father had been the son of Mazlund, by a mortal mother, Sombra. But we all have a Mazlund-in-us, she thought.

"What we have is a compact that states quite simply that our actions and decisions must be for the common good, the well-being of all of us. And what we have is love. That is the quality we must recall when the Mazlund-in-us summons another response. We have experienced love. All of us. And it is always available to us. It is that availability and our willingness to avail ourselves of it that links us to the larger power, whatever we in our debate about terminology choose to call it. It is there. And, should we doubt that, remember that Mazlund knows it is there and constantly tries to subvert it. But when we recall the constant presence of that larger power through love, we defeat Mazlund every time, no matter where he chooses to abide moment by moment."

She paused.

"We will place a granite obelisk on the spot where Glorimere fell," she said.

"Yes," said Neutralon, "and it will say, 'Here rests Glorimere, Queen of Archerland, loyal to the last.'"

"Yes," Estrella said. "We must remember that we, as a people, fell from the Living Lord. For whatever reasons, we fell to admiring our own reflection in our mirrors, not recognizing that our images are merely those of animals who can think, who have learned to think, who have been given the grace to accept a power larger than ourselves, a dominion greater than that of our own mere minds. We cannot invent some self-serving parable that claims that the loss of our island kingdom was just a natural event. It was more than that. We were not open to the warning signs. We had closed our minds and erased our contact with the larger truth that is – and here we pause before the mystery – beyond this natural world. We must remember our past in both its greatness and its shortcoming, celebrating the former, but knowing that the latter can occur again if we are careless, unheeding, forgetful. We do not control history. We do not control nature. At best, as we have learned here in this wilderness, we cooperate with nature. And, if we do, we cooperate with the Will of God. We have learned that, have we not, even if we cannot explain it?

"Please recall, my countrymen and natives of Otherland, please attend to the Second Book of Judges – that passage familiar to some of you about the Angel of the Lord who had chastised the Children of Israel. 'Ye have not obeyed my voice,' said the Angel, representing the point-of-view of God. The Angel said that their enemies 'shall be as thorns unto your sides, and their gods shall be your destruction.' And, as we have learned, if we do not obey the one true voice, our enemy will set up a competing narrative that will lead us astray. Several stories can exist, but only one can be true for us of Archerland. But we cannot merely say, here it is! We are in the process of discovering it and in that discovery we perform the work of God in His Kingdom. And even there we discover other stories, like those of our brothers and sisters of this new world. Because that is where we are. And now, Neutralon..."

Neutralon stepped forward and looked down, as if seeking the words in the grasses at his feet.

"Powers that surround us, no one can be neutral. Still, we can be wrong in what we think is our rightness. Help us to know your wishes. Let them flood past our own and take us with them. Help us see in our darkness. Help us listen in the noise of our daily lives. Provide silence, Living Lord, so that your word can be heard. Help us remember our dreams, when you have entered from our own depths, from the God-in-us who makes of us much more than we are when we believe ourselves to be awake. We have made a new beginning here. Let each day be a beginning. Keep the pathway clear before us as time moves forward as well and as temptation would pull us from the way. Guide us, we pray, in such ways that your will becomes what people who come after us will call history. Help us to tell your story. All of this we ask in the name of God. Amen."

And so, for the time being – the only time there is — the survivors of Archerland and their friends, the nation headed by the wise Umgalla, had time to breathe, to build permanent structures for the refugees, to tell stories and compare the evolutions of two different peoples, now joined for the purposes of fellowship and mutual support, to educate their children about the ways of words, woods, waters, and winds, to recall and repeat their modes of worship, to grow the corn and wheat, hunt the game, catch the fish that would stead them during the winter, and to wonder about Mazlund. He would return. The question was – when? But for now it was a good time. The earth gave up the heat it had stored in the early summer, and the waters near the mainland grew warm, and the stars crackled above, in the clarity of summer nights. They looked cold, out there in that depth of sky, but they were warm as the earth poured out the warmth it had embraced, and they spoke of good things, perhaps merely speaking as themselves, perhaps articulating the voice belonging to the unimaginable vastness of the light behind the dark canopy, of which the stars were the merest suggestion.

And they stood there as the sounds of battle echoed away into history, amid the quiet that the wind drop at sunset brings. They watched, as rising from dark shoulders of storm that had held lofts of piled thunder along the west, a rainbow rose.

Neutralon bowed his head again. The others also did so.

"Thank you for this sign of peace, Living Lord and for this promise of a covenant renewed. Amen."

Yes, Estrella said to herself, thank you! Now, she thought, I know it to be true!

The survivors of Archerland and the citizens of the nation led by Umgalla said, "Amen!"

Postscript

Estrella ruled wisely, as was her wont, having few decisions to make, few disputes to adjudicate, heeding the voices of her people. She watched her sons with pride as they grew into men.

Neutralon became the reader of prayers for his people and delivered the sermon of thanks when the harvest was bountiful and the fish of the sea plentiful. Since that was a frequent event, Neutralon had to prove inventive to keep his audience alert. He chose to mention specific fruits, vegetables, and fish, the better to make his congregation hungry. He also enjoyed his role as schoolmaster for all of the children of Otherland.

Jerome the Gnome and Lisle continued to be happy together, particularly since Jerome continued to find the most succulent mushrooms in Otherland. Thanks to Umgalla's counsel, Jerome never returned with a toadstool.

Tomaso the Troll contributed in many ways to the good of his comrades and learned to savor living in a community after so many years in the damp darkness under a bridge. His eyesight was never particularly strong, but his insights were incisive.

Grunius learned to decode the signals of Otherland and found mostly fortunate prophecies in the hieroglyphics made by trees against the horizon, clouds against the sky, and stars against the night. He founded the discipline known as cryptography and the technique known as Variable Image Sequencing (VIS).

Cybella befriended the resident deities of pool and grove and learned of the natural history of Otherland, talked with Grunius, walked among the trees, conversing with them in almost inaudible murmurs, and enjoyed her garden. Her spinach was especially successful, and she insisted that Grunius eat his share of it.

Majorum and Harry were married by Neutralon and, in the years that came, enjoyed their stalwart daughters and sons.

Gregg and George worked together on the boat and supplied the colonists and the natives with supplies of fresh fish and succulent shellfish to supplement their meat and vegetables and fresh fruit in season. They built a smaller type of boat called the Seawing (recognized by the gull wing on its sail) and, in the summers, conducted races within the sheltering arm of Cape Discovery.

Umgalla continued to rule wisely and at last left the land to live with his ancestors.

Seraman settled into his better nature and discovered that the invariable good humor of his persona was who he really was.

Chirac enjoyed helping Grunius as Assistant Chef and Chief Birchbark Steward. For the first time in his life, he liked those whom he served, and, for the first time in his life, he served willingly.

Reeps was happy to cooperate with his new friends on projects a bit less grandiose than Mazlund's attempt to outdo the splendor of Solomon's Temple. Reeps was responsible for the splendid causeway that links the Lake of Midnight Music with the village that the Archerland survivors and Umgalla's people built, on the basis of Reeps' design.

Blackie spent her nine lives with the sapience she had learned from her yellow-eyed ancestors of the Nile.

Sheba proved a trusty ally to the survivors of Archerland and, with the help of an intelligent wolf who served the people of Umgalla, produced a breed of wonderful dogs known as Otherlanders. These dogs learned to read single words on hand-held cards, a talent that proved useful in situations demanding silence.

Hector retired as a guide to the Afterworld and was reunited with Andromache on an island near where Achilles lived. In time, the two warriors became friends and enjoyed an occasional evening trading tales of the great war in which each had fought on opposite sides.

And Mazlund waited. After all, he has eternity in which to wait.

Printed in the United States
200815BV00017B/26/A